F. LOCKHAVEN
REECE MATTHEWS

Editors
David Aretha
Andrea VanRyken
André MacLean
Grace Lockhaven

TWISTED KEY
p u b l i s h i n g

2021

D1571244

First Printing: 2021

ISBN 978-1-63911-007-0

Twisted Key Publishing, LLC
www.twistedkeypublishing.com

Ordering Information:
Special discounts are available on quantity purchases by corporations, associations, educators, and others. For details, contact the publisher at the above listed address.

U.S. trade bookstores and wholesalers: Please contact Twisted Key Publishing, LLC by email twistedkeypublishing@gmail.com.

Contents

ACKNOWLEDGEMENTS

Reece Matthews, thank you so much for your incredible help bringing this story to life. Your insights and tireless devotion to this book were invaluable.

I also want to thank our beta readers, Nikki Boccelli-Saltsman, Christine Mattila and Elisabeth Allen—who also came up with the awesome title *Saving Garlic*.

Thank you to our editors David, Andrea and André for all your patience and great feedback.

And to our amazing illustrator, Jelev, thank you for all your patience and for creating an extraordinary cover.

I

Fashioned into an attempt at a road, the bog, filled with muddied waters, was nothing more than a recreated moat. On either side of the mound of dirt was land… and its potential wasn't what it had once been.

Indeed, this side of the town now seemed surrounded by its own self-contained murky atmosphere. Its dirt roads ran the gamut between glistening-wet to a full-blown slough before the swampy nature of the surrounding scenery left nothing but a sour taste in both mouth and sight.

Yet a group of teenagers and children still ran through this run-down side of town with a skip in their step and a smile on their faces as they crossed the manmade bridge of dirt—essentially a hardened hill that was paved over until it wasn't anymore—for their game.

Most knew this side of town to be under the weather—or some form of a bad spell—and whilst it was home to some unsavory groups, it was misjudged and abandoned, for the most part, making it a peaceful place to romp through.

No border guards stood present on the other side of the failure of a moat, which was now a terrible drainage system. So, the group was allowed to run free into the nearby swampland, more akin to a watery forest than anything else. Still, the group didn't care, running for their lives as if this were the last game of hide-and-seek they'd ever play. With their faces filled with bright, beaming light, their bodies filled with adrenaline, and their hearts pumping blood a mile a minute, they continued their game.

They ducked, rolled, and chatted in erratic, worried patterns with the group slowly splitting off into various factions. Some of these sub-groups were mixed in their social backgrounds while others stayed within their family boundaries. The land was theirs to play with, use, and adapt, and they did so, though in places they muddied their boots and dirtied their worn clothes to various shades of brown.

One girl—who had foolishly thought a white dress had been a delightful idea at the beginning of the game—didn't let the wet surroundings stop her from lying low among some bushes.

And then came the call.

He was coming—the seeker. The oldest of them— a young man in his own right, tanned, with keen eyes, ruffled dark locks, a tattered top, and equally distressed bottoms—stood ready. He ventured outward, his feet left almost bare save for the shallow excuse for tight-fitting caligae that he wore.

He prowled across the land bridge and failed moat and observed both sides in wonder. *No, they wouldn't dare tread in all of that,* he thought. Not even *he* dared traverse the makeshift sewer system.

He continued onward, eyes moving across the road and the enclosing trees. The marshland beyond obscured all else from his sight. He knew there were open patches here and there, where forest wetland and marsh became an open bog. He knew the land well, being the oldest of them and native to this area. So he decided to move to the left side of the road first.

He knew he had missed the group, who had taken the right side of the road and migrated toward the other side of the marshland. Still, the left side was safer. He knew someone would be foolish enough to take the left side of the road as the marshland was denser, and posed the chance for a better hiding spot. The marshland as a result was far more dangerous in his memory, so to think anyone actually went across the left side of the road left him worried.

He heard the youngest child of the group snicker nervously, and in his shock, he spun and pretended he heard. He knew where they were and smiled before mumbling an incoherent thought to himself. The last thing he wanted to do was follow the giggles of the group who were less serious about the game. To find them so soon would ruin the game for them.

His mind *clicked* as a win-win scenario presented itself. He chose then to leave the group amassed within the shrubs of the tree line on the marsh's right side and near flung himself into a brisk pace toward the leftmost side of the marshland.

They get to enjoy playing the game more, and I can gather whoever chooses to take the dangerous parts first before something stupid happens to them. Last thing I need to worry about is fishing someone out from the bog, he thought. *I'll play it easy for now.*

He turned left and continued on his way, marching through the shrubbery of the land and sticking to the familiar footpaths. The problem for those who tried to hide here was that if their steps weren't well-placed, it would likely make a clean, brand-new, and easily recognizable track. Sometimes, this worked against him. Today, it worked for him.

The left route into the marsh held the dangers of tripping over upturned routes, being stuck in the bog's firm hold, or simply the wildlife, which seemed more fervent here. The last thing he wanted was to learn that a less-than-grateful otter had its home trampled on and was about to respond with sharp claws and unpleasantly terrifying teeth. The thought of a toxic toad or poisonous frog lingered on his mind. By the end of those thoughts, he wanted nothing more than to be rid of the marshland. He wanted to find those who took the route.

This was the first time in a while since they last got the chance to *all* play hide-and-seek together. He expected nothing less from the bravest of their group than for them to try and outdo him by risking themselves in the clumpy bog.

Their plan would work on any other seeker—anyone else wouldn't dare come out this way, he assumed. But him? No, he was more than prepared to risk the deeper, darker part of the marshland if it meant a victorious game of hide-and-seek. Besides, his brotherly instinct for the group was as strong as if they actually all shared a legitimate blood-bond. He refused to carry back any helpless teen who sprained their ankle on an upturned tree root.

Little do they know, I'd rather find them first so they can get back to safety before I leave this area for good.

He kept onward, noticing some breakage in some bushes, an odd tree or two that had a branch snapped, and other areas in which the land had been disturbed. His grandfather hadn't instilled all that hunting and tracking training in him for nothing, and he used it well as he caught sight of a white mass moving between the shrubs.

"Cassandra, you know I can see you, right?"

The white mass froze.

He smiled slightly. "I can see the mud on your dress. Won't your mother be upset?"

A slight grumble echoed out from her direction, followed by the shuffling of shrubs. "She'll buy another."

"Not without you receiving a good punishment first," he pointed out, crossing his arms. From the shrubs came a young girl, slightly pale in skin with her ginger hair tied up in a bun. Her blue eyes gleamed with frustration. "How did you find me first?"

He casually gestured to her white, flowing dress that dropped to just below the knee. He wasn't quite sure how she had gotten it so messy. "White stains, doesn't it?"

She snorted as she maneuvered toward him. "Sort of...."

Cassandra fought off a stubborn branch that tugged at her dress, and for the slightest moment during which her dress snagged backward and tightened to her frame, he quickly averted his gaze from the slimness of her form.

It had always eluded him before, but right now, he found politeness overtaking him. He preoccupied himself with the branch not far above her head. *If she were any taller, she would have had to pull it from her hair instead of her dress*, he thought. He looked back at her, musing over how tall she was for a young lady....

"Got it," she mumbled, victorious against the tree branch.

"Nineteen years of age, and you can't beat a tree branch?"

"Be quiet, you," she retorted after a short-lived laugh. After she won that fight, she turned back in his direction with a hefty grin. "I'm the first one to be found, aren't I?"

"Maybe…," he shrugged. "Depends?"

She gave an odd smile. The unspoken game of flirtation began as it normally did. It was often a private thing when moments like these occurred. When just the two of them could speak freely and as equals without the teasing of others. She often preferred to not dwell on it, but for him, it was the perfect opportunity.

"On?" she finally asked.

He gave a short bow. "If you'd be so kind as to direct me toward where your group is."

"My group… *team*… is none of your business."

"Oh, come on," he began and twirled around on the spot. "At least make it easy for me." His survey of the surrounding area was complete and he saw nothing but marshland. No one else was to be found.

"Like you need it easy," she teased and slowly brushed by him. "I swear, every time you try to cheat, another freckle comes up on my face."

He gasped. "Was that self-mockery? That's rare from your cut of cloth."

She knocked his arm lightly. "Just for that, you're not getting a helping hand."

"Just for what?" he said, playing dumb.

"You just made a reference to my background."

He smirked. "What's wrong, rich girl?"

She didn't frown or glare. Instead, she only stared with an inkling of affection for his raillery.

He met her eye—a buzz of romance passed between them as he turned away. "I'll live with my choices."

"Darn right you will," she stated, stern but playful as she continued on her way. "I'm on your team now… but don't expect me to be helpful."

He looked over his shoulder as Cassandra wandered off. "Wait," he called and spun to watch her leave. She was following his trail, heading back the way he had arrived. "Where are you going? We're a *team*. Did you forget what that means?"

She stopped. "I'm going to keep guard to make sure no one tries to escape back into town." Cassandra crossed her arms and turned to face him. From a distance, her cocky glare met his. "How about this: If you can spell 'team' perfectly, I'll give you a hint as to who is around here."

"T-E-E-M." He stood tall and proud. "There."

Cassandra shook her head, then theatrically rolled her eyes and tutted. "Ah, better luck next time. I'll grieve for you."

For a moment he was confused. Then it clicked in his head. "All right. Touché."

She flashed him a small smile. "Careful what 'cloth' you try to contend with, Michael."

"What's that supposed to mean?" Michael's face drooped into oblivion. "What cloth?"

"It's a reference," she explained, exasperated. Through a sigh, she explained mockingly, "a reference to what you said about my 'cut of the cloth.' Now, I'm poking fun at yours." She turned away from him for a moment. "So, what I'm *saying*, is don't mess with me."

Michael, honestly lost at this point, merely assumed she was flirting. "And you, Cassandra—"

"I've told you many times before, it's 'Sandra.' Got it?" She threw him another glare, then smiled and went on her way without another word. Her slip-on black shoes, coated with mud, trod on through the stable marshland around her. What was left of a once-polished, metal strapped and laced pair of shoes, was now a shadowed, muddied version of its former self. Before long, the mud would dry and crust away with every step. He wished she'd give more care to her clothes, as not everyone, including himself, was so lucky to even have shoes, let alone good ones.

Unfortunately for you, you've already given me everything I need, he thought to himself with satisfaction. *By saying you'd give me a hint, you've told me what I most needed to know—that someone is still around here.*

He ventured deeper in, ears open and eyes steady as he minded his every step. He knew that Cassandra wouldn't dare go too deep, but there were others who might.

He wondered if perhaps Luke or Christopher was hiding somewhere up ahead. He bet it was Christopher. Then he thought, *No, they wouldn't dare go this deep.*

A gentle panic ebbed in his heart. He knew what kinds of creatures might be dwelling within the shrouded shrubs around him. Go too deep, and one of them might take notice.

They should be fine within the radius they had decided upon, though. This wasn't their first game out in the unknown. Yet, he feared the worst as the warning of responsibility was in question.

He considered himself the caretaker of the large group. Being the oldest, after all, came that responsibility with that exact task of looking after the others. He thought to himself as he spun. *And they are old enough to be brave and stupid.* He couldn't fully dismiss the thought of something dangerous happening, but he didn't believe they would be so foolish as to invite trouble.

He reminded himself that any kind of animal could be lurking out there. It only pushed him to move quicker and find whoever was left out here. He'd rather not have a fight with the wildlife. His mind considered the possibility of wolves—or worse, lost and desperate brigands and thieves.

Michael smiled, for he stood at the very edge of the safe zone and slowly began to turn. *Knowing those two, they're likely circling me. Teenagers make for good fools sometimes.* He assumed, maybe, it was the twin pair instead. The power duo—Andrew and Sophia. While the two were courageous enough, he knew that even they wouldn't push the boundary too far. Or, at least, not so far that a dying scream could not be heard....

He frowned. *I shouldn't have brought up the game of hide-and-seek.* He considered the twins to be an interesting pair, to be sure, but knowing them... well, Michael only needed to look to the trees, and....

He stopped.

The area was silent, other than the noise of his hitched breath. He saw a faint bit of scrappy fabric, one that he was familiar with. A touch of mud was on the torn piece of clothing; it was a small piece but familiar enough to identify.

He let out a gruff sigh as he straightened and reached with all his might to touch the fabric stuck in the tree. Though he was fairly tall, the tree's height just outmatched his. On his tiptoes, he stretched up toward the branch the fabric was draped over. Wet, muddy, and fresh. The cloth had recently found its way there. The color was too strained, too hidden, to be seen properly. He tried to leap for it once and then a second time.

A sound.

"Andrew?" he murmured. A light patch of sweat grew under his armpit. "Andrew, out of the tree, will you?" He turned slowly and caught the teen hanging unhappily from a branch across the pool of discolored water. Michael chewed the inside of his cheek and gave him a disappointed look. "You're better than this."

"So are you. You can't just keep asking for us. We're never going to reply."

Michael shrugged. "That's only in previous games we've played. I know better now."

"Are you sure?" Andrew retorted, partly cocky.

"My instinct is always right, though," Michael replied, casual in his response. Carefully, Michael tried to traverse his way across, but the ground was growing damp and unstable. "Andrew, have you got a safe path back?"

"Not while I'm in this tree."

"He tried to help me!" a shrill voice sounded.

Michael froze and glared at Andrew intensely. "Is that Scarlett? I swear to God if you put my sister in a tree, *Andrew….*" The ripped, small piece of clothing on the other tree made it clear. Andrew had tried to help his sister into a tree, failed, and rushed to another one.

"She wanted to follow Sandra. That's all, I swear!" The young teen, blond and messy, was wearing the same grin that seemed permanently plastered on his face at all times, yet he somehow managed to express the compassion of a protective older brother. "Come on. She's not that young either. She wants to have fun—"

"She's *eight*."

Andrew let go of the tree and dropped down with a *thud*. "W-well… you…." He went from landing flat on his back to crawling on hands and knees to finally rising to his feet. He then spat out, "You w-were hunting at her age, right?"

Michael glowered but loosened up quickly. "That doesn't matter. It's not her age I'm concerned about…," Michael fastened a stern gaze on Andrew. "It's the person looking after her."

"That's rude," Andrew blurted out. "Besides, I found the best tree. Why do you think I stopped with the one you're at?"

Michael's stern look turned to the tree Andrew had failed to get Scarlett into and then landed back on Andrew. The tree, in Andrew's favor, was fairly thick at its base, but the branches and any climbing potential were bare of options. The tree seemed too good to be true—something Michael understood Andrew had learned after Scarlett had already torn her clothes on a branch.

"I got her down safely…," Andrew's voice petered out.

Michael pieced two and two together with the ripped clothing and noticed where it was torn not from Andrew's clothes but his younger sister's.

"Did you try and get her in a tree?"

"To be fair to me, she was the one who climbed first." Andrew, sheepish, passed a glance to Scarlett. Hidden behind a tree, little Scarlett peeked her head out to see her older brother. Michael's eyes focused on where a piece of her clothing was torn. It was minuscule, but enough to be noticed with a concentrated look.

"Clothes are hard to come by, Andrew." Michael narrowed his eyes. "It could've been worse, I guess," he said and looked at Scarlett who seemed a mix of shy and happy to see him. A part of him didn't mind if she wanted to take a courageous route.

"Honestly," Andrew began quickly, nervous as Michael got closer. "Either she has no fear or has no awareness of danger!"

"That's beside the point," Michael replied with a glare and a relentless tone. Michael's concern was noticeable, but it passed.

Andrew had Scarlett—a sweet, young girl, clothed in tatters and rags—kept nicely bundled in Andrew's makeshift jacket as if she were wrapped up in a blanket. Giggling, she waved to her brother, who softly waved back. He was appeased.

"All right. Well," Michael said, forcing a smile, "I've found you both. So, get back to the road, okay? I've got to stay around in case you are hiding anyone else out here."

"I'll get her back safe, I promise!" Andrew knelt and took her hand. "Come on, Scarlett. Let's go find Sandra and the others!"

Excited, Scarlett happily bounced along with him, and the two of them were once again off on an adventure together. By the time they were long gone, their voices faded away, Michael realized that if Andrew was here, surely Sophia was too? Or at least… Emma. *No, Emma wouldn't come this far out. She wouldn't put the effort in.* Cautious, he placed each new step down as carefully as the last.

The swamp was thick, the marsh grew deep, and the bogland moved further away the deeper he got. He kept to the outskirts, following little bridges of land, but soon found himself at what he believed to be the limit. In his mind, the only person to have come this far out had either already left or been caught. Andrew was, at least in his mind, the only person brave enough to venture this far out into the marsh.

Shaking his head, he turned back, carrying on his way. He retraced the same trail he had used to travel this distance, moving more quickly now that the path was clear and already before him.

Stumbling his way back to the place where he had caught Andrew, he called out, "Sophia, if you're here, you should know I am leaving and probably won't check here again. So, come back, will ya?" He didn't expect a reply and could only hope she heard his call and would follow secretly behind him.

Sighing, he walked toward the little lost wooden stump once more, his eyes crossing the branch with the now-missing piece of his sister's torn clothes. He swore it had been there only a minute ago. It was gone.

He nodded and looked behind him. "Sophia, don't you dare be playing games with me." Nothing. "Or… Emma? Maybe… wait, did Abby come today? I didn't get a good look at everyone who joined the game." He felt a ball of anxiety grow in his chest. *Oh, Abby, I swear…. You better not have come out this far out.*

"Abby?" he called out gently to see if the young teen was in the surroundings. A muffled noise sounded. "Abby?" he tried again, hoping to retrieve and help her. "If you're there, I'd rather not leave you out here alone." He heard no other noises so he continued forward.

An otter passed by, ignoring him, and then continued on its way with a piece of muddy cloth in its mouth. Assumption confirmed. He was happy to conclude at that point that no one else was present in the area.

His journey back—until he met the road—was spent pondering whether the others in their group went to the other side, where the bogland grew more extensive the further out you went, or if they returned to the first district. Unsure, he carried on his way, moving onward down the road....

He stopped abruptly.

Eyes narrowed, he moved to the opposite side of the path. Whilst he had chosen to venture off to the left side of the road first, he knew that most would have taken the right side. He considered the right side of the road, and further out in that direction, to be the safer route. Nevertheless, he knew why he had chosen to take the more mysterious off-road route first: to make sure no stragglers ended up lost or worse.

He stopped again.

He swore he heard something. Words. Talking. A muffled voice that tried to stay soft and secretive.

Michael's naturally silent approach aided him greatly as he neared the vicinity of the conversation.

"Oh, they are quite sharp, aren't they?"

"Well, I wouldn't lie. Now, if I may...?"

Michael moved closer, and a thought crossed his mind. The voice he heard, though muffled, clearly didn't belong to anyone who joined the game today. If it was anyone he knew, it might be Brandon, he thought. Suspecting Brandon was a fair assumption, though he swore the young man was working at his father's blacksmith today.

Still, Michael wondered if the sight of him at the blacksmith's workplace had been a ruse, and Brandon had secretly gotten involved with the game…. The voice alone was more masculine than anyone else's, and the only other person near his age was Brandon, after all.

Slowly, he moved off-road and down a small slope, silent on his feet as he found the tracks toward a small, bunched-in gathering of bushes, branches, and finally… not the two individuals he expected.

He found Sophia, the energetic, happy-go-lucky wild card of their group. Though he couldn't see her face, he saw the back of her head, highlighted clearly with the sun beating down on her. It was the man next to her that made him go still. Instead of rushing to action, Michael stayed calm and quietly asked, "Sophia, who is this?"

2

"He won't give me his name." Sophia popped out from her hiding spot. "I bumped into him while trying to find the best hiding spot. He was already there."

The man shook his head. "This hardly counts as a worthy hiding spot," he replied and slowly revealed himself from the bushes. Because of the heavy layers of robes, tatters of cloth, wool, and various stitches of jackets and coats, the overly clothed man showed no skin other than his face with a wrapping of cloth around his head and a scarf around his neck. He looked as if he were homeless, but the scarring and burns across his face, tanned and dark, left him charred-looking. "Please don't mind me, I'm just passing on my way through this town."

Michael stopped him. "What is this town?"

"Alvia," the strange man answered.

"No," Michael answered and gestured for Sophia to come to his side.

"No, Michael. He's really nice!" Sophia protested. "I didn't think so at first either, but it was funny when I scared him and he told me not to spook a vampire!"

Her protest was noted by Michael, though he didn't care for it. Her argument regarding the strange man seemed logical enough, at least, until Michael's brain clicked.

Vampire?

The man sighed and shook his head. "Young girl, I trusted you in confidence when I asked you to please not say a thing."

"It's okay. We can trust Michael," Sophia assured candidly, her expression cheerful as she wandered off back toward the path. "Don't let him in the sunlight." She turned her head long enough to warn Michael, then giggled and let the two be.

Michael, frozen, felt his knees buckle. "I… you… *no*."

"It's okay, young man. If you don't want trouble, I shall leave and try another day…," the vampire turned away and then back toward him. "What is this place again?"

"Uh… this is Alvina…. My proud…t-town."

The vampire gave a curt bow. "Alvina? I see." He spared a short glance to the side. A small hum expelled from his lips. "I'm sorry to have bothered you—"

"Alvia was a witch," Michael clarified quickly. "An ancient one."

The vampire shot a glance at him. Something in his eyes screamed "curious" about Michael—and perhaps of all things. Michael gulped down his fear and stared back at the stranger.

"Ah, was she now?"

"Y-yes…."

"Strange, isn't it, to name a town after a witch?" The vampire considered this, then seemed to brush the notion aside. "I suppose… it hardly matters. After what happened in Salem… when was that now? It must've been at least a good 150 years ago now. I… think. My memory isn't as everlasting as my life." The vampire leaned forward. "So… the witch's name was Alvia?"

Michael nodded and paled. "Yeah…. They say she owned this land. Then the people came and took it. They say that's why this side is more… uh… poor. The farmland and beautiful grassland are on the other side."

"I see. Where did the witch supposedly live then?" The vampire's innate curiosity began to creep over Michael, and he shivered. "Or did she live on the farmland?"

"I don't… k-know. I… I work on the farmland. Always looked too beautiful for a witch to want to settle." Michael scratched at his clothes—which more resembled rags.

The vampire nodded, unsure. "You'd be surprised…. Not all that you believe is evil requires "evil" sights and smells around it. I suspect if she were a true witch, she would have settled here for access to the marshland's properties." The vampire let loose a small gasp. "I've over-spoken…. Please, ignore me."

"It's okay."

The two locked eyes for a moment.

Michael shuddered. The stutter from his voice began to lift. "I.... It's okay. I don't know if the story is true, but it *did* lead to the divide."

The vampire nodded. "I don't know either." He looked down on Michael. "If she were real, I would have hoped to have met her." Michael watched as the vampire's face puzzled out a thought. "I've heard of the divide here. I was led astray, however. I assume my previous informant thought I meant the ancient witch." The vampire looked around. "Well, if that is all...."

"And they *burned* her, they said. The tales make her sound so horrible. But they say she was nice, you know? A good witch."

"Ah, I see. She couldn't have been a witch then." The vampire's face, which had at first seemed so grizzled, appeared soft now, yet taut. "A witch is hung first, then burned. Or... *pressed.*" The vampire recoiled. His reaction was brief but noticeable. Michael swore he saw something. A hint of... emotion.

"You... uh, oh. Witches aren't put to the stake then?"

"Most are," he answered and began to move away.

Michael stepped forward. "I-I can't just let you go."

"You must."

"I can't. What if you try to hurt someone?"

"And?"

Michael gulped. "And steal their... blood?"

The vampire shook his head. "Of course, I chose to come here looking like a wistful blanket, to find my prey in the most out-of-view, out-of-sight, out-of-mind, backward part of town, using a road that isn't commonly used nor known for easy access."

Michael, bemused, merely nodded. "Uh, yeah."

The vampire stood and pondered too. "Ah, yes, that does make sense."

"Please, don't kill anyone," Michael pleaded.

"I wasn't going to." The vampire scrunched his eyes shut. "I just wanted to easily pass by the town is all."

"Promise?"

"Uh… promise."

Michael put his foot down. "See? Why don't I believe you?"

Groaning in dismay, the vampire lurched toward him slightly, terrifying the boy into a statue. "I wanted safe passage. I planned to hurt no one, but the land becomes too open and easily seeable in certain parts, and I hoped not to fall into the trap of being seen as I know the town is on high alert… on the other side."

Michael bobbed his head up and down. "Uh…," he cleared his throat and shifted uncomfortably. "Yeah, that's the 'posh' side," he said and mimicked an overly dramatic accent. "And they sound all like *this, and so lovely, and so sweet, and so…*," he smiled.

"They are quite nice, actually. People are just super-stitious here, but they are quite lovely."

"Indeed. The girl didn't scream."

"Sophia."

"*Sophia*. And you haven't either...."

"Michael."

The vampire glared. "Do you think me uneducated, boy?" Michael shook his head. "Good. Now, my plan was to slip through the town, if possible, as going around would not only take too long, but in my eyes, the belly of the beast would likely be less weary than those who are actually tasked to be the watchful eyes on the outside. As I move through the city, it gradually gets nicer and prettier with the swampy, murky land turning to grassland and into more of a pretty, managed forest on the other side. It's a whole... plan. Now, if you want to know why I am telling you, it is exactly for this reason—I just want to reach the other side without anyone trying to burn me or shove a stake through my heart. Though, let me tell you, a clean swipe at my head with a sword works just fine." The vampire, agitated, took in a deep breath as Michael took a step back.

"Oh, really? I would've... never guessed." Michael pondered quietly, and so did the vampire. For a brief time, the two discussed what might be the best way to go about killing him, though the vampire remained vague and quickly changed the subject.

"I'll be off, then. Have a good day."

"You can't just leave," a feminine voice said sadly, and the two men turned, aghast, to see that Sophia now rounded up their group. Michael wanted to smash his face into the tree. The vampire wanted nothing more than to also smash Michael's face into the tree. Now, he had far bigger problems than just one girl and a young man.

"Please, keep it quiet!" Michael begged to no avail as the group excitedly approached whom they called the "Kind vampire."

Well, if he wanted us dead…, Michael looked at the strange vampire, *…we would be.*

The group, alarmed, swarmed the ragged, blanket-wrapped vampire with a luscious desire for both knowledge and glory. To them, it was truly a wonderful thing to meet such a supernatural creature. Michael couldn't believe it. It wasn't real. It felt too acted, too sudden, and yet the brimming curiosity of the group overtook any potential fear they had of the vampire.

They don't actually believe he's a real-life vampire, do they? Michael paused in his thought process. *Wait. What if he has been playing me for a fool too?*

"How do we know you actually are what you are?" Michael asked, his voice rising above those in the group to get them to calm down.

"I… I don't know. My teeth, maybe, but it's not as obvious as you think—"

Andrew leaped forward, and on his lips was the largest, most mischievous grin he had ever shown. "Do you know any wondrous people?"

"Wondrous people?"

"Yeah, like, other creatures?"

The vampire faltered. "What could you possibly mean, child?"

"Like, other mythological things. Come on, you're a *vampire*, aren't you?"

The vampire scrutinized the boy. From the grubby white pantalettes, the poor fabric shoes, and the front-buttoned tunic covered by an old Eton jacket, he saw the details of an individual with a mixed personality. He'd lived long enough to recognize the earnest curiosity and foolishness in Andrew's eyes.

"Just because I'm a vampire doesn't mean other mythological creatures are real, and if they are, I'll bet they are nice people. I haven't encountered any, truly, in all of my time of being alive."

The group, quiet, waited as Andrew led the charge, circling the poor man. Michael sighed and wished for the ordeal to be over.

"He's just homeless," Cassandra said, looking him up and down.

The vampire shot her a look and nodded. "I won't argue with you on that." She was far more taken aback by his agreement than anything else, and his words seemed to water seeds of trust in the group.

"You don't have a home?" Luke—a young boy with tussled black hair, begrimed clothes, and a little bit of chub to his cheeks—asked, revealing his bubbly personality. "Wait, where do you live?" he inquired next.

"Are you hungry?" little Scarlett asked. "Vampires get hungry!"

"All right, Scarlett," Michael began, trying to intervene before they were all killed and harvested for their blood.

"There's no way there's nothing out there," Andrew pressed, saddened. "Nothing at all?"

The vampire grumbled, "Honestly, I am still waiting for the day some sick human creates something as disturbing as Frankenstein's monster."

The group considered and protested that remark.

"No, Frankenstein's monster is a 'creation,' whereas you were born!" one of the children pointed out.

The vampire, hands held high, protested as calmly as possible, "Look, children, the world isn't all that you hear. There are no monster hunters, no vampire clans, no fighting warrior, tooth fairies, apes with advanced technology, or bartering leprechauns—or even unicorns who'll never let you ride them because of their doggone pride. Or demon-possessed mino-taurs rampaging the land while angels battle occult-ists in the skies above!" The vampire, slowly, came back down from his erratic speech. The group, shocked, watched as he calmed. "W-was that too… much?"

"Some of those examples felt far too specific," Cassandra argued, and slyly added, "Honestly, some of those sound as if they *are* real after all."

"Or *was*." The vampire, voice gruff, shook his head.

"Was?" Cassandra repeated.

"Humanity," he answered, making his point clear. "Humans were the reason for the perishing of crea-tures that were once just a normal part of life and the world, now made fantasy."

Sophia softly retreated from the situation with a slight, poor grasp of the reality that the vampire had made clear and was now known and accepted by the group. It overturned a lot of what she thought, and now, a new perspective formed. Though, she was not the only one among the group who had a shift in their perspective and heart toward the vampire.

"Except for those doggone unicorns…. Don't travel too far south, will you?" Andrew beamed at the vampire's words.

"I was… uh… joking," the vampire clarified.

Andrew pouted and puffed out his cheeks in anger at the stranger's betrayal.

Was he joking? The unicorn one sounded a bit personal, Michael thought curiously. More than anything, he now wanted to inquire further, but the vampire's exasperated rush to speak convinced him to stay quiet.

"Besides, I wish it were all true, that I could meet things as strange as I. If they are anything like me or live as I do, they likely just want a friend." The vampire stepped away. "So, I must be going."

"You want a friend?" little Scarlett asked sweetly.

Though his skin was burnt and tanned, it became clear that somewhere in what was exposed of his face was a rosy blush.

"I… little girl—"

"What are you?" Sophia quickly interjected.

Standing tall, the vampire looked over the group. "I sense none of you intend to harm me…. You said before about how mankind's 'creations' don't count. Well, I was cursed and created; nothing more, nothing less," he finished, while the group seemed enraptured by his story.

"Um… anything else?" Emma asked gently, a girl who stood nearly as tall as Andrew but didn't share his knack for extroverted talk.

"No," he replied.

"Nothing at all?" Brenna—a teenager with pitch-black locks and black skin, wearing a hunter's garb for their game of hiding and seeking—asked.

Some would say it is too much. She often says she is fitting the part. Michael nodded in approval of Brenna's dress code.

His shoulders drooped. "What do you want from me? There's no special background, no brilliant story. Life isn't all mystery sometimes. More often than not, it is because a man falls in love with a sorcerer's wife, and she falls in love with him. Then he steals her away, so the sorcerer chooses to curse his bloodline. This all resulted in... well, me."

The group, shocked, began to feel the blooming buds of reality—he might indeed be a vampire.

"And... does this mean your bloodline is cursed?"

The vampire offered a smile to Cassandra. "Well spoken, young lady. Yes, and I refuse to fall in love or have children as I will never put my curse onto them. It's selfish." A saddening moment passed, with every last person affected regardless of how young he or she was.

"So... so... is magic real?" Andrew asked, his eyes flickering with interest.

The group began to bicker. The danger of the subject left a heavy toll on all their heads. Both fear and wonder filled them. Every last innocent member in their company was stuck between the reality and the truth.

The vampire knew what he had to say could be dangerous; though, having come this far, he wasn't about to turn back now. He mustered up the courage. He was prepared, as they were, to break down the reality they knew. Though, the worry of what might happen should they talk about it to others was a risk to them all. Then again, he'd lived long enough to know better than to flee and leave them hungry for knowledge. More often than not, it led to a harsh outcome with their controversial questions being shared with others around him.

He felt a part of him sink in shame, though only for a moment, as he knew that his discovery meant one thing and one thing only, he'd have to educate them before they got themselves prosecuted by any religious figures of the town.

"Keep what I have to say to yourselves, I beg you, for this world won't be kind to any of you…." His eyes scanned the group of girls, mixtures of hairpieces straightened or curled their hair into a bun. The boys' hair was kept short, though there was the odd case of ruffled locks or overgrown curls.

"Is it real?" Andrew pressed on with his question.

"Oh, gods, yes, it is." For some reason, the vampire was taken aback when the group happily began to discuss magic, only to remember they likely shouldn't do that in open, lest they become suspected of something.

"You said you wanted to get through the town, right?" Sophia walked toward him and joined him at his side before addressing the group. "Everyone, I met him first, and I know he's safe. I think he is a real vampire. So, we're going to play a bigger game of hide-and-seek. What do you all say?" The cheerful response from the group was a start. Sophia nervously continued in a bumpy tone, "G-good.... So... we're all going to be on the same team, and we're going to get him through this town no matter what, okay?"

The group quietly murmured back and forth, mostly among the older members whilst the younger members were all for it, having decided the vampire was indeed nice.

The group at hand were an odd bunch. The vampire liked that, how the group's age was so perfectly mixed. The younger members of the group had donned shirts, dresses, and blouses that ballooned at the sleeve and waist outward. Their garb held a unique blend of patterns and colors; from white to red to brown with a dash of black here and there, the various shades all complemented one another where possible. The faded shirts and grayed buttons were bone and metal. Ankle-high laced shoes or pull-on boots covered their feet; some also wore hosiery. Some of the older boys had a cap shoved mostly into their pocket, whilst many girls kept a maiden's hood draped around their neck. The clothing varied between loose and close-fitted, and the older children had mostly switched to trousers, vests, and jackets whenever possible. It fascinated him to see how fashion had evolved over the centuries. It was something he knew he'd never get tired of.

He swore one boy had fall front trousers…. They were slightly torn, but overall, his apparel had maintained its quality.

The group began to close out their discussion.

"Wait, where's Scarlett's cap?" asked Michael.

"I'm in," Andrew said, and slowly he was followed by everyone else until they all stood behind the vampire.

"Good." Sophia looked behind her and toward where the group and the vampire were, then she faced Michael.

They all stood there.

"Sorry, but has anyone seen Scarlett's cap?" Michael's question again went unanswered.

"Children, you do not have to do this," Abby said, and despite her being among the shortest in the group, save for the young Scarlett, the pale girl with short brown hair did the one thing she was best at—scaring the group half to death for a moment by her sudden outburst right before laughter erupted around them. None had seen her standing among the group, silent and carefree. She was often considered a ghost of the group, being so quiet and shy but also so unpredictable.

Michael gave up. "My father's going to be real upset when he learns I lost Scarlett's cap...." He turned to Abby. "We are, though. We are going to help this, uh, vampire. Anyone who would rather not be a part of this is welcome to go. Otherwise, well...," Michael confirmed to them and himself, controlling the situation, before he said with half-hearted confidence, "we want to help."

They continued to stand there.

The vampire sighed. "If this is a game of hide-and-seek, then do know that you need to lead and direct me as if I were a pawn on a chessboard.... I don't know the town's layout."

Michael stepped forward, hoping to avoid the disappointment he felt in thinking the vampire would lead them. He was the only actual adult of the group, after all. "All right, everyone, let's move out and create a formation around him, with the tallest next to him so we can keep him covered, got it?"

"*Got it!*" the group hollered.

"Too loud!" Michael hissed.

"Got it!" the group hissed back.

3

Michael bit his bottom lip as the group tardily moved toward the dirt road. He looked at the vampire, who offered a smile. "Don't worry, this isn't the first time a younger generation has shown me open-mindedness. Please, go ahead. Direct me. Also, it would benefit me greatly if you could tell me about the town."

On their journey back to the dirt road where their group amassed in both secrecy and a growing improvised act, Michael explained how this side of town was denser, cramped, and run down. Compared to the favored religious buildings and possibly ancient monuments on the opposite side, his area of the town was poor and criminally run, mostly.

On the outskirts of the town was an area more akin to an old town. There, the group saw older buildings constructed from perhaps the last one hundred years or so. The density of the buildings began to space out more as they continued their trek. This "old town" section was positioned slightly beyond the growing, old shantytown. Wooden homes and shallow huts made for a poor sight.

Though, as the marshland fell behind them, and the dirt roads, muddied sidewalks, and the up-to-no-good looking fellows who often spared a curious eye to their group, Michael's mind began to slip into a sharp focus.

The vampire's did too. He thought of the Gothic style and its rare sightings. He almost remembered when such areas had flourished in the late Middle Ages. Though there was rarely a Gothic home in view, as the slums were a distant memory, he noticed where strict protection had been placed on smaller churches and the run-down cathedrals of old. Old and in need of renovation, definitely, but preserved all the same. He'd always admired the defined features of that style, from the pointed arches to the rib vaults, buttresses, and all-inclusive usage of stained glass. This town seemed far lesser than he expected despite its show of such old architectural grandeur. Considered and then brushed aside, he ignored the reminder that such a town was old but had only in recent generations found a boom in people.

It's not been long…, his thoughts rambled onward. The sights in view were few but still enough to remind him of the days when Westminster Abbey was first built. He had briefly passed through London and seeing it at a time before its various run-down periods and renovations was a memory he hoped to hold onto. Like most things, such a memory only came to him when prompted.

He smiled, though, for a voice in his head told him to thank the French for bringing much of that architecture to England in the first place.

England...? he thought. *I thought it was only recently they called themselves the United Kingdom... Ah...when was it...?*

Onward into the town, the group moved in a melodic pattern, and though there were few around, their awkward movements alone caught eyes. Yet most shrugged them off as "kids being kids."

They continued to move as a group, with Andrew leading them slowly but steadily and gradually employing Sophia to kickstart a conversation to get the group engaged in something other than shuffling nervously—especially the younger children, whom he feared might begin to overthink at some point and panic.

Gradually, Andrew shifted their group to move more on the sidelines. Though it was messier there, none of them cared, for they had already ventured into the swampland.

All the while, the vampire continued to ponder about his past and whether it was here or in mainland Europe where brick-and-stone-styled architecture was more common. It wound him up. Drove him mad. He couldn't place his finger on it.

Was it...? Ah, it's Prussia now. Denmark has been as it is for a long time. Hanover... that's what it's called right now. That's where the more distinct style was. His thoughts left him with a grim smile. *To think it wasn't long ago that the Holy Roman Empire collapsed.*

"Are you okay?" Michael asked.

"Thinking." The vampire looked at him. "Just about how the times change.... You'd think I'd be tired of it, but somehow, if I don't at least appreciate the change, I think I'll go insane trying to remember what once was." The vampire sighed. *To think back to the days before even that.... By the gods, I don't remember it well. Europe has always been a cesspool of conflict. No better today than how the Romans fought against the barbarian advances from Germania.*

"Don't get too distracted," Michael warned, voice low. "Your daydreamin' is making you a lousy hider."

The vampire collected himself and brushed off the memories of the past.

As they neared a turn, they saw the shift ahead from the deep outskirts in the "Old Town." For most of them, Old Town was also home, and as such, filled with potential dangers—such as being caught by parents, extended family, or other acquaintances.

"Andrew, isn't that your mother?" the quiet but posh voice of Cassandra warned, watching the familiar slender woman—about a block away—walking toward their group.

"Yeah, that is." He gulped. "Right, this way, then."

Andrew, moving quickly, directed the group to turn and rush in the other direction, hastily forcing the vampire down a cramped alleyway where the group muttered and giggled and worked together, keeping one another safe while acting as if they had evaded threats that they actually hadn't.

Then, there was the vampire, who constantly wondered if he should have trusted them.

Oh, these…. Ah, what was it again? The Tudors. No, inspired by the Tudors. Tudor-inspired houses. From what narrow view he had, he tilted his head, unsure. *Does it hold the signature Tudor arch… or at least curvilinear gables?*

"Hey, don't be dawdling!"

He wasn't sure who said it, but he knew he needed to heed the words.

No, those were reserved for the wealthy….

"Come on!"

The shouted whispers brought him back to reality—a reality similar to the one the group had long since realized, he assumed.

They were escorting a vampire. And any punishment, if caught, wouldn't be endured easily.

If he was to be caught, he knew he'd have to pretend he mind-controlled them or some such magical crap so the town's people wouldn't sling them up on a cross or stake, much like they had to the supposed "witch" the town had seen who knows how long ago.

"Do you transform?" a rough voice whispered loudly in his eardrum. The boy in question was fairly tall with brown eyes and brown hair—all a mess and yet somehow groomed. He dressed no differently than Michael, barring the use of a tunic, of all things…. He wondered how long it had been since he had seen such a garment.

"Transform? Sorry, what? Who are you?"

"I'm Chris. Call me Christopher. No, Chris." Their movement in the alleyway ground to a halt as Michael handled some unknown issue up ahead at the exit.

"So, do you?"

"Surely, this isn't the time."

"There's no better time."

The vampire met his eyes, glared, and then huffed. "Do you children feel no fear?"

"I'm *fifth-teen*, thank you."

Yeah, and I'm…. How old am I? Whilst an existential crisis dawned on the vampire, Chris continued pummeling him with questions, while on the other side, Abby—who stayed at the rear—endured having to listen to Chris spout out more pointless words.

"You must get what I mean? It's like an angry face. Like, you transform when you become evil and angry, and you just…become evil-looking, right? All horrible and screaming and bloody. Like the fairy tale stories my dad reads me."

"Okay," he began with a loud whisper, "one—those aren't fairy tales, those are horror stories, and two—I am a vampire, not Satan."

Chris nodded once, then a second time. "Abby, what do you think?"

Abby quietly whispered, "Just shut up, Chris."

Chris spun away from her, nearly tripping in the cramped space. "Okay… you don't have a monster face? Are you boring?" The vampire glared. "C'mon?"

"Bit picky, aren't you?"

"I'm a bit of a nitpicker, I admit. So, the idea that muscles rearrange themselves in the vampire's face to give it a wicked look is just… a myth?" Chris looked to the ground. "Everything is wrong. It doesn't make any sense to me. Why would they put it like that in the books then?"

"To make him look bad!" Abby vouched for the vampire, who wanted nothing more than to try and figure out what Michael was dealing with without either of them getting caught.

"There's no excuse for it. You're boring."

"*Chris!*" Abby chided.

"But he *is*, Abby!"

"Look, I'm a monster with a human face. All right. It's all to trick you into trusting me. Does that quench your insatiable thirst for truth, child?"

Chris nodded. "Yes… and I am fifth-teen," he asserted a second time.

"I… I…," the vampire died inside. "I know…."

"He is right, though," Abby chimed in.

Oh, by the gods, not her too….

"Do you not have to put on some special face to drink blood? Like, do you rip your lips and jaw and get all bloody and gory?"

"No… I might tear my lips a bit for the bigger folk, and that's it. It doesn't look scary. It makes me look like I have chapped lips, and it's sad." His lie passed, and he hoped the addition of a bit of dramatics to it would quell their interest.

The two teens nodded in unison. "That is sad."

A moment of silence was offered. Their reaction wasn't what he had hoped for—

"Wait, is that true?"

Great….

"No, the size of a person doesn't matter. Sure, sometimes I have to open my mouth wider, but it doesn't tear my skin nor jaw."

"But you do drink blood?" Chris persisted.

"How else would I survive?"

Chris pursed his lips. "Okay, nice."

Nice? These kids… ugh.

He wished to focus on the architecture, even if only for a minute.

Turning away from the two children, who were still bickering, he looked ahead, feeling jaded. Michael shifted outward from the cramped space, exiting the alleyway at last. He watched curiously before their cramped queue began to move.

The child in front of him, quiet and shy, couldn't meet his eyes. "Uh, I...," she began.

He looked at her, curious as to who she was. In his mind, she was Emma, and she had a question, but the bravery to ask it didn't quite come until the person in front of her started moving, and then she was quick to scamper along too.

Avoiding whatever she hoped to say, he ignored her, his focus on reaching the end. One by one, each child was ushered through the alleyway and out into the shaded, open sidewalk.

"Andrew, Cassandra, Luke, Sophia, Scarlett, Brenna, Emma, *person*, Christopher, and Abby.... That's it, I think."

Person? The vampire looked at Michael, amused. *I won't tell you my present name, or any of the many names I have used in the past. I'll let you decide, lest you recognize one and hear the tales of the suffering I've caused.* He then attempted a confident stroll along the side of the path, shaded by overhanging pitched tents and the makeshift balconies of increasingly pleasing-to-the-eye homes, until the vampire felt a firm grip on his wrapped elbow.

"Wait. Hold on," Michael directed, gesturing to where they should wait for Andrew and Cassandra to secretly round up their group around the entrance.

"What's the wait for?"

"The locals want to know why such a large group of teenagers and children are going through a back alleyway." The young man let go of his elbow and kept his tone fair but low. "I just want it to seem natural as if I'm getting everyone out."

"Seems reasonable," the vampire replied, remaining steady as he shared a smile with a passerby who was quick to jog along, his pulled-back grimace at seeing the supernatural creature's face evidence enough of his repulsion.

The vampire, understanding that they didn't want more eyes on them, wondered if anything bad would come from him trying to smile at a stranger as if he were truly normal. He wondered if perhaps smiling randomly at strangers wasn't exactly normal either. He cursed himself. Despite his longevity on the ball of dirt he called his world—his hell—he was amazed at how often his social interactions left him reeling inside, hopeful to escape and forget humans forever. Sadly, he often never forgot the awkwardness he could cause.

"Cassandra?"

The vampire turned toward the firm voice, belonging to the young man who towered over the group—though they hardly seemed to notice him at the moment. Michael grabbed the vampire's side and tugged him forward, with Chris and Abby following in pursuit to keep him covered. Further out from the alleyway and the surrounding high-top roofs that extended outward from the houses, the sun began to glare down on them.

"Stop, stop!" the vampire nervously muttered, fighting back against their forceful maneuvers. "Not too quickly," he warned, keeping his head ducked to avoid the incoming light; his skin beneath the layers of rags felt warm from the sun's threats. Looking back, he saw Cassandra walking alongside a man who was questioning her. His persistence was clearly causing her annoyance.

Her father? The vampire took in the scent of the man. His essence, the hint of his blood…, he shared the same scent as Cassandra. *No, surely not?*

The man looked nothing like her. His slicked-back ginger hair frolicked in the breeze, thick and clean, whilst the rest of him was accompanied by the wealthy attire of a burgundy jacket and high-class clothing. The vampire nodded to himself. The sight alone said enough—this was her father. He had to be.

When his eyes crossed the group, the vampire saw them grimace and stiffen and knew the truth—she was the daughter of the town's head of law enforcement.

A single memory flashed in his mind.

"Be careful of Alvia's overseer. He's the mayor's right-hand man. He'll have an emblem of sorts, made of engraved silver… the shape of a lion's mane and face."

He studied the emblem adorning his quality-rich jacket. The glint of the light, reflected from the sun, glanced off the silver emblem and shot dangerously forward. The vampire spun to avoid its glare.

He was thankful for his informant's warning at least.

Within mere seconds, the vampire felt a tug at his gut. The law enforcement official approached the group with slow steps; he was tall and lanky, but lean compared to his daughter, whose frowning face made every last freckle appear sad.

"Do not let him see me," the vampire warned, knowing why the man was there. He was on patrol for a clear reason. The official likely knew an un-wanted guest might choose to travel through his town. *I'll assume you were tipped off to my whereabouts. I must proceed, sir, no matter what.* The vampire had a mission, after all.

4

With careful movements, the group surrounded the bulky, clothed man who kept his head low, beads of sweat dripping from his exposed face. The sun was like a predator, and it begged him to look up, even if for *just* a moment.

"Cassandra, please, you're covered in mud."

"I was just playing, Father."

"Playing?" His voice was stern and had a brusqueness to it. It sounded forced, but the vampire guessed it could be made to sound pleasant if he were in a good mood. His dirtied daughter now standing among an unsightly, *different* class of adolescents no doubt painted a picture in the father's mind he'd rather not see. "Playing with whom?" The father knew the answer to that too; he was merely delaying the inevitable.

"These are my friends," Cassandra argued, the area around her and her father gradually clearing of bystanders. Their voices alone left a negative aura around them. The friction between the two grew, and the look upon Cassandra's face signaled something the vampire was unsure of. He knew how to read a human; he had been around for long enough to know such an expression well. The girl didn't seem afraid or worried, and if she were, it wasn't out of the risk of his discovery. He saw instead a hint of carefully hidden woefulness on her cheeks, lips, and eyes.

She had something to hide.

When Cassandra rang out in protest against her father, who now clutched at her wrist in despair, he tried not to stare and attempted to let the crowd of children shuffle him to safety with the guidance of Andrew. Though he was concerned that their efforts were in vain.

Cassandra fought against her father's strict touch; he was firm, his waxed face, slick hair, and pristinely plucked eyebrows with the accompanying affluent attire was his way of embracing his calling to the flush life. He donned pinned medals like a veteran of war, though his waxed, smoothed face looked like it hadn't ever seen a day of combat.

"To think that your mother and I truly believed you were going out of your way to learn the acquisition of a thespian. How have I never seen this till now?"

"I've known them for years," she said and fought back with spite. "You just never cared enough to ask."

"Or do you play out of my view?" Her father scoured the faces in the group. Even the youngest knew that the implications that look passed along weren't kind. "Do you play in the backwaters of this town? Do you go to the marshes?" He pulled her close, his grip on her wrist leaving a hot, crimson marking. "You lied to your mother and myself."

Michael stepped forward. "Sorry, sir. We were just playing—"

"Do *not* speak to me, young man," he answered back with an agile fury, yet it was clear he was confused above all else now that his anger had subsided somewhat. "Cassandra," he began as his crew of four men, soldiers in their own right, began to fan out around him. Their focus, however, was on Michael. "Why are you loitering with a boy such as this?"

"Man," Michael uttered quietly.

"He's my friend," Cassandra answered, bland in voice, though she was troubled in everything else.

The vampire watched on, eyes narrowed, curious.

"We're just playing games."

"Such as?"

"Hide-and-seek...."

Her father wrinkled his nose, glaring heavily at Michael as if he were to become the scapegoat for his daughter's playfulness. "Across the town with this boy and that... *lot*?"

"*Father!*"

He lamented a spoken curse under his breath and cast a look across them with no attention to their individual details; he didn't even care to study their faces. "Sweetheart, you told your mother and me that you were at the theater—"

"I *was*," she lied convincingly. "But I just got caught up and wanted to play, that's all."

"You shouldn't lie to us, nor should you associate with them." He looked specifically at Michael. "Or him."

Michael shied away, visibly hurt.

The vampire watched on and saw something deeper in Michael's eyes than shame. He was truly hurt. Was it the father's words that struck him so, or was it something more? He wondered how, for years, Cassandra could have gotten away with things her parents clearly did not allow. He wondered if her parents were too lax, or if she was just a really good liar. The situation asked questions only Cassandra could answer, and she had nothing left to support her case of lies. She accepted her father's grim words, though he did nothing more to scold her.

"Go on," directed her father.

"W-what?"

"Go home." His demand was clear. Cassandra turned toward the group and then back to her father.

"*Now*, not when you're done playing with ruffians."

Cassandra didn't dare look back or say another word; her act of defiance was to rejoin the group and urge them along. Her quiet grumbles to keep them moving were done with malice. Escaping the situation was an easy feat for her to obtain. Explaining her side of the story to the group who looked at her as if this were their first time learning of her tension with her father would be a more difficult matter.

Have you been living two separate lives, young lady? The last thing he wanted to do was underestimate her; however, her reasoning didn't matter. Her lack of honesty on both sides had created a drama of social class, and he, the vampire, just wanted to get across the town.

He didn't want this. Oh, how in his heart did he wish he had tried to take the long route despite all the risks it posed.

As the group shuffled and marched, the vampire felt himself spin back, curious, as he met the father's eye for a split second—a second too long, yet also enough.

He saw the flintlock pistol with its ivory stock on the law officer's hip.

The vampire shuddered. *Oh, how I despise such weaponry.*

"Just keep moving," Michael said, voice low and dark.

"I'm sorry," Cassandra said to him and him alone. It was sudden and quick. She meant it, of course, with all her heart. She looked at him and hoped to meet his eye. He didn't dare meet hers.

The vampire saw the exchange in clear view; it was sudden and sharp. And whilst most shied away and said nothing about it, it was Michael who appeared to be shadowed and wore a dark look as if the reality he once knew was now broken.

"You're a rich girl in silk and lies after all?" Michael's words were spoken lightly. "What do you have to say about that?"

"That you need to listen to me first," Cassandra shot back at him. "Just listen before you say something stupid."

"Stupid. Yeah, that'd be me, wouldn't it?"

The two locked eyes.

The atmosphere had already shifted.

"Silk or not, I—"

"Muddied silk," he added.

The vampire furrowed his brows. He wasn't sure of the intention behind the two words. Whether it was for the fact that her dress was literally muddy or because the muddied silk was some kind of metaphor…. Then again, was Michael intelligent enough to think of something like that? No. Maybe. He felt bad for that judgment and remained quiet.

"At least she has silk," Sophia said. Her comment, out of place and unneeded, somehow propelled the group into an ignorant bickering.

"Well, if you weren't out here helping the… *person*," Andrew retorted, "then maybe you'd have silk one day too."

"I don't want to be a seamstress like our mother!"

"We should respect her!" Andrew kept his nose high. "Our dad is a tailor, after all."

"Hardly." Chris chuckled. "He's a lower-end one, at that."

"Say that again, will ya?" Andrew grumbled.

"Oh, I will."

"You two! This isn't the time," Sophia intervened.

The vampire noticed only now how much the group differed by the rags Scarlett wore to the wool clothing that covered the rest of the group—excluding Andrew and Sophia, who seemed to have more unique attire made from linen and wool. It was only Cassandra, though, who appeared truly different. A silky white dress was bound to stand out.

He thought, then, of how he stood out too. A heavily clothed, bandaged man…. His gut began to worry.

A sense in his soul warned him of an impending threat.

As the group bickered, he began the hunt for the danger. With his eyes, he saw little, but an eternity of instinct honed his senses. His ears heard every last trace of noise, whether it be the crumpling of gravel beneath feet, an uneven cough, or the gentlest of whispers among the crowd, he heard everything.

With such senses, he felt his nostrils adapt and the hunting instinct begin to surface. It kicked in with a fury. The scents of everyone around him emerged, a unique ability of his own, of his curse, that allowed him to trace and track the trails of his prey. When combined, he alone could feel his senses align in the right direction. *The militiamen.*

It was that flintlock pistol. Ever since he saw it, it loomed heavy on his mind.

I refuse to be shot, he decided, panic rising inside him.

"You can't say anything anyway, Andrew. You shouldn't be out here either. All you boys should be out on the farms, shouldn't you?"

Better the farms than the workhouses. The vampire closed his eyes. *I'm happy they've been spared some of the terror that the industrial menace has brought on this world.* He opened his eyes. *And to think, the worst horror they can imagine is me when their technological thirst will end them…. These kids should be innocent of it. Alas, this is an odd town in an odd place. It's been spared, it seems.*

"Yeah, well… do you think I want to wear a smock?" Christopher argued. "You should be happy yer father's a tailor."

"Stop arguing!" Abby's meek voice broke out.

The boys looked at her.

"What? You'd rather go home and sew and knit for the rest of the day?" Christopher crossed his arms. "At this point, we're all as bad as each other."

The realization clicked in the vampire's mind. "Are you all avoiding work?"

Silence.

"That answers that."

"At this point, we're using you as an excuse not to do our chores," Cassandra chimed in as if nothing within their group had splintered.

"Well, more so us lot. What exactly are you meant to be doing otherwise?" Michael stared at Cassandra. Her return stare was blank. "Do you have work?"

"I… my parents want me in the arts. I try… I'm *learning* to sing and dance and act. Though, the acting is more of a… well, I do have acting lessons, but it's more of a *was*. I go so little now that I'm surprised my teachers haven't brought it up with my parents." Cassandra crossed her arms for a moment and then uncrossed them. Her discomfort spread to the rest of the agitated group. They hadn't really moved from the alley since her father's intervention. Since then, the town seemed all the busier. "I've got piano lessons, too."

"Good for you," Michael said in a cold, calculated tone.

"Thank you." Her reply wavered as she began to realize their friendship wouldn't have as smooth a recovery as she had expected.

It's all downhill from here, young lady, the vampire thought.

"Okay, then. We're all in agreement that we're all terrible people?" Andrew waited for the group's agreement, which came eventually. He nodded. "Well, that settles that."

"May we continue?" the bored vampire muttered. "The town only grows more lively."

"Yes, let's go." Michael gestured to the group. "If it weren't for *her*, we'd be halfway across town by now."

The vampire wrinkled his nose, curious as to the truth of the drama, but knew no answers would present themselves at the moment. He suspected there was more to Cassandra than met the eye.

Swinging back, the young lady kept her head high and continued to direct the group.

"Cassandra," a familiar voice called out again. "*Cassandra!*"

The vampire knew that voice. The father had already called out to her again. He presumed that what the law official, Cassandra's father, wanted to know was why a bulky fellow—with only his lightly burned face revealed—was currently with a group of children.

A man who was tanned, burnt, and bandaged from head to toe while wearing rags and mixtures of cloth was sure to appear out of place. He knew he was going to attract eyes sooner or later; it had just been a question of what pair of eyes caught him first, and he knew from the menace in those eyes, and who they belonged to, that as the group began to scatter toward

the incoming crowds of a hectic market, it was run or
die.

5

The stench of fish left an unwanted tingle in the vampire's nostrils. Wrinkling his nose, he tried to rid himself of the smell. There was no escape, though, as he bit the inside of his cheek and listened patiently on the sidelines to two young adults arguing about things that leaped between subjects. Cassandra, at odds with Michael, argued about their next move. Their group was shattered, and its members split up into the on-going market.

Cassandra whipped her head to the vampire and spoke rapidly. "Please, stay low. We'll regroup in the central square!"

Michael blurted out with rage, "The central square? Do you *want* him to get caught?"

"No, Michael. Please, we just need to focus on him."

"I *am* focused on him!"

Though it seemed fair to be upset with the girl who had tried to live between two worlds and had thus created a middle ground lie, the vampire knew Michael's thought process was not helping right now. The two bickered head-to-head with no hint of recon-ciliation in sight.

The vampire fumbled his way away from the fish stall, its owner casting concerned glances toward the arguing pair. The noise of the market drowned them out for the most part, and the crowd at the fish stall left them fairly shrouded too. Thus far, it seemed their hunter wasn't on their tail, but as to the rest of the group, they didn't know.

The lack of coordination between them left them vulnerable. The trio may be safe for now, but he knew any number of their friends might have been caught. The last thing they needed was for the town's guard to use them as bargaining chips.

"We need to split up. Can you handle that?" Cassandra asked, a firmness to her voice.

"Who put you in charge?" Michael retorted roughly. The implication of his anger wasn't lost on either Cassandra or the vampire.

"What? Is that too much for you?" she snapped.

"There are bigger things right now—"

The vampire, caught between the two young adults, felt the hostility rise. He waited for the two to decide on their next course of action but knew time would likely not provide them a chance to argue it through.

"We should try the outskirts of the town. It's safer," he decided, waving his hand across the air at the girl, who flinched.

"And what? Get caught by the border guard? Even if we could make that choice, it would take far too long, and the night guard is just as strict."

"It's safer," he countered.

"It's not."

"It's the best route for him."

"*Not anymore.*" The vampire saw the entourage of her father come into view, along with the red-faced man himself, who rushed between every last individual who bared a resemblance to anyone in the group or the vampire. "Argue as you will," the vampire said and raised his hand in the direction of her father. "It means nothing as long as indecision holds us in its grasp."

As her father tailed them, curious as to who the hefty, clothed homeless man within their group was, their time continued to be wasted. He wondered why the man was on such high alert.

The town's busy market attracted people he believed to be far stranger than him. Was it the circumstances? His association with his daughter and her group? Or was it that the law enforcer was aware that an assassin was coming through his town? The vampire bit the inside of his cheek and avoided pondering the matter further.

"We can't have my father alert the Lord of the Town. If he does, we'll never get him out of here alive." Cassandra stared at Michael who remained silent. "We take the inner route, got it?"

"As long as you're telling the truth."

Cassandra spat back, "And what does *that* mean?" She knew exactly what his sly tongue had hoped to rile up in her heart.

The vampire, however, had already slipped away, having chosen her plan as the best route. Quickly, he mingled with the crowd, and from within it, he noticed using short glances that the rest of the group now bounced between locations, having not run as far as he had expected. His attuned senses singled them out speedily. They seemed lost without Cassandra or Michael to lead them.

When they saw him, they sprung up from their places and bolted, scattering into the market and moving among the crowds with ease until, one by one, the group became fractured and struggled to remain clasped together.

Dangerous was the town market that ripped them apart, and ruinous was the central town square where crowds focused on a preacher of the church who provided a public ceremony the vampire wasn't accustomed to. The wooden stage and podium nested various criers, men who'd cry out the daily news and the word of their God. They took their turns, and the news of the day was made clear for all to hear. Their distraction provided his getaway.

He looked at the architecture, saw the gorgeous hint of the Renaissance poured into every last elaborate design, pattern, and structure. He saw the clear fenestrations, vaulting techniques, and open truss designs of the Elizabethan-style buildings. The town grew and changed with time, it seemed. Its town center and central market certainly boasted their architectural ability.

He spun toward the distant view of an English Baroque-style city hall. Politics and policies were at play. People argued there, and the numbers of folk flowing in, out, and all around it was significant. So much so that he felt overwhelmed by it all.

He missed the days of old when the world held fewer people in it. It was a strange, almost eerie thought. Yet prosperous men dressed in frock coats and tall silk top hats were all around. From their linen pullover shirts with full sleeves to their deep, buttoned cuffs and generous collars, they were everywhere.

Women in frilly dresses that ballooned outward.

Children with caps atop their head who laughed and dashed from one place to the next.

Merchantmen with very long fabric tails tucked into their trousers to save them the pain of the scratchy wool.

The odd few who still had knee breeches that he swore had already passed from fashion's good taste a few years ago....

Everywhere. So many people. A swarm. A crowd of madness.

He couldn't.... He just....

He froze.

A gentleman of financial wealth saw the still vampire and expressed his concern to him. It all was but a blur, though. All he felt was a numbness, and what he saw remained a blur—until his view began to stabilize on a singular man in finer fabrics with furred ruffles at his sleeves and neck. His vest revealed a silk damask, and when he stepped forward, his fine leather boots *clapped* against the cobbled ground. The man reached for him.

The vampire knocked his hand away, pushing away his help.

All he saw and felt at that moment was the way the world had changed.

It wasn't the first time, and it certainly wouldn't be the last.

Recently, though, times felt as if they were changing far, far quicker than normal.

"My apologies," the vampire muttered, and in his sorrow, he ran. Fled, more like. Almost like a confused rat in an obstacle course filled with people. The man moved on, it seemed.

The vampire pressed forward.

Focus. Focus. Focus…. Focus…. Don't stop.

"Vampire!" a hushed, sweet voice called, and he nearly barreled into Scarlett. With rosy cheeks and a playful smile, she tapped his upper thigh. "Vampire." She gasped, barely reacting as he scooped her up in his arms and flung himself toward the outer edges of the central square.

In his view, through his sight and hearing, he sensed the whereabouts of the other children moving to and fro, all with the hopes of finding him and avoiding the prestigious man and his soldiers, who had begun to hail more guards.

"*Vam*—"

"Scarlett," he interrupted, hasty and concerned, "give me a nickname, and that'll be my name, okay?"

"A nickname…," she thought deeply, so deeply that she was quiet enough for him to slip toward the exit where he saw familiar heads bobbing toward and outward from. He presumed the exit he saw was the one to take.

"Do you have one?" he asked.

"What?"

Staying to the side, in the shadows, he stopped long enough to scour the area. "A nickname?"

"I'm thinking!"

"Okay, okay," he uttered, uncaring to a degree. He just hoped she wouldn't keep saying "Vampire," as it only took one wrong ear to hear it, and all would go down in flames.

"No," she said sadly. "I can't think of one."

"I hate garlic. Use that, or something." He stopped, surveying the area and the bypassed shopkeepers who noticed his panicked movements.

"And you are old?"

"Am I old?" He wasn't sure what she meant.

"Are you?"

Am I? He thought. "No… not really. But, yes. Yes, I am old."

"Like, super-old?"

"Yes. *Now—*"

"Like, an old man? My dad calls me a junior." Scarlett tapped his head as he spun, trying to find a way through the crowds who continued to amass to hear the preacher. The more people who stopped moving to listen, the more obvious he became. He was aware of the mounting danger he was in and wasted not a moment more to being stuck in it.

"That would make me a senior, then?"

"*Yes*," she gasped, astonished. "You are Garlic," she decided proudly.

"That's it?"

"Yes!"

"My nickname is Garlic?" He rocked his head from side to side. "It'll do."

"But an old piece of garlic."

He internally died for a moment.

"Like…," Scarlett rested against him. "Like Garlic Senior?"

"And… that's my name now, I assume?" *I'd have preferred just Garlic.*

She hummed, growing distracted by the preacher whilst the disoriented vampire held her. He navigated his way toward the exit and kept her safe all the while. At least, until she started happily prying at his make-shift tattered turban.

"Excuse me," a woman began as he nearly slipped through the exit, "are you okay?"

"Yes, yes. Just—"

"Not you, the girl," the woman clarified. Everything was moving too rapidly for Garlic Senior, his grasp on reality wavering as he feared being caught out, if not for being a vampire, then for something else... something worse. "Are you okay, darling?"

6

"This is Garlic!" Scarlett's proclamation made the lady step back.

"Oh, o-okay?" she stammered, unsure how to handle the beaming little girl.

The vampire nervously smiled. "My niece certainly has quite the imaginative mind, doesn't she?"

"Y-yes?"

"Well, I am late for… my…," he looked around. "Rehearsal at the… church. So, goodbye."

"Wait," she called out as he rushed away, Scarlett bouncing up and down, laughing as they went. "What role have you taken on?"

"Uh, it's a surprise!" He spun around a corner and slipped away from the central square. The crowds thinned and snippets of sunlight bounced off his cheeks, leaving that gentle searing that he had never gotten used to. He moved toward a corner where the shadows were aplenty and saw that an open area down the paved, cobbled road was a blacksmith. It took him a moment to realize the town gradually was becoming nicer and more reputable. It took a moment longer to notice Michael nearby chatting with two people.

What in the world?

Michael appeared distracted, nervous, and happy all at once. He had caught up with friends, it looked like, or so Garlic hoped.

Muscular and stocky, a young dark-skinned man stood opposite the downcast Michael and talked with a great sense of bravado. He either hid his emotions well or the other wasn't good at noticing them. Running a hand over his short-cut hair and stubbly scalp, the new face took a moment to laugh at a comment the younger of the three of them had made. Casually, he patted his darkened, dirty apron down before scowling at his gloved hands, which had just dirtied his head. Even from a distance, Garlic could tell his voice was fair and smooth instead of deep, which Garlic would have assumed would come from the throat of a young man of such stature.

His eyes drifted to the overzealous giggling of the smaller, younger girl with them. Skinny, wearing garb that was one size too large for her, was a young girl with the apprentice blacksmith. The conversation at hand was open and far too easy to eavesdrop on. They were essentially catching up on each other's lives when Michael and the man named Brandon shared another laugh at the blushing expense of the girl called Cari, whose name had dropped in a conversation Garlic had overheard. He stood on the sidelines, listening intently.

"See? She has not one or two sisters. She has *three*. That's *three* generations' worth of clothing hand-medowns she has to go through." Brandon gently nudged Cari, who nearly attacked him in return. "What she's wearing now is probably at least twenty-five years old." Brandon slowed his chirpy tone and let loose a few chuckles as he took in the ominous presence of a strange man holding a little girl. It took him a second to recognize Scarlett, who continued to try to peel off Garlic's turban.

"Scarlett?" Michael said with a voice that dripped with bafflement. Across the paved-stone path, he advanced on Garlic, who, grumpy, slowly tried to hand the girl over. Her protest left Michael with a grin and Garlic with a frown.

Now I'm going to have to keep holding her....

"Who is this?" Brandon asked, looking over the tanned, heavily clothed person who tried his best to stay in the shaded area of the adjacent building's balconies. "A new friend of yours?"

Michael hummed, then went quiet as he tried to think of something clever, though the progression of that thought clashed with the sudden slowness of his brain. "Yes."

Garlic's frown deepened.

"We named him Garlic," Scarlett announced.

Brandon's amusement at Scarlett's proclamation caused him to cross his arms, muscles strenuously bulging with force, only to quickly relax them again. Garlic knew the young man had briefly considered intimidation but had chosen at the last instant not to go that route.

"You look like a dried prune," Cari commented, squeezing in between Brandon and Michael. "Like a roasted prune."

"Don't be rude," Brandon said plainly, "and don't judge too fast either."

Cari watched him carefully. "He looks nothing like garlic!"

"*He's here!*" a young voice shouted nearby.

Me, Michael, or them? Garlic turned as a swarm of frantic adolescents approached with a fury, voicing their concerns over how they lost him and how they feared he might have died or dried up.

The vampire smiled, due in part to the fact that their game of hide-and-seek across the town had gone so terribly. He saw well enough that the group didn't truly realize the stakes of the situation nor what might happen if they were caught. Still, they swarmed him with joy and questions.

Knocked into, nudged, and shoved, he struggled not to be urged into the sunlight or anywhere else that might attract outside attention.

"How can a man work with all this noise?" Deep was the booming voice that he at first thought came from Brandon. Instead, it emitted from the throat of an older man, almost an exact replica of Brandon in his attire and stature. "And who keeps going on about garlic?" The old man entered the fray, much to the annoyance of Michael and the disappointment of Cassandra, who had also joined them. Neither shared any direct interaction at the moment, though now that time had told the truth of what they felt in their hearts, Garlic could see Cassandra's stubborn dissatisfaction and Michael's saddened, tough shell. They were at odds with one another, though he swore at first, he had sensed a bond between the two.

"Playing games across town?" he asked, burly and tall as he looked them all over, knocking into his son playfully as he went. "Brandon, you've worked hard today. You're welcome to join them if you want to…," his voice trailed off as the attention of the bickering group turned to him. "Is this little Scarlett?" he asked, then slowly moved near Garlic. "She's growing up quick." With a smile, he turned to Michael, who exasperatedly agreed.

Scarlett mentioned one more time that the man who seemed made of heavy cloth was named Garlic. She smiled.

The father stopped and paid closer attention.

Garlic met his eyes and put on a fake expression of innocence, which turned into a mix of a grimace and a smile. He looked desperately at Michael.

I don't want a fight, please.

Michael stared back at him; his eyes showed how dead inside he was.

Young man, do something...!

"And, who is this... *man?*" asked Brandon's father.

Everyone, silent and nervous, looked to the next person to answer until slowly but surely, the matter rested on Michael's shoulders to deal with. He pushed his thoughts for a reply, and in his plight, he turned to Brandon, gently pulling the teen back enough so that they were out from the father's view, who unknowingly chatted with the group's most conspicuous individual—the star player in this improvisation of their situation. Hiding Garlic's truth was the priority.

"You owe me that favor, remember?" he whispered to Brandon. The father didn't hear, but Garlic did.

Relying on these new faces? You'll have no choice but to involve them, and I don't want to put more of you at risk.

"Get us out of this, and I promise I'll explain," Michael continued.

Brandon raised an eyebrow and scratched his stubbly jaw. He wasn't pleased, though that didn't stop him from dropping a confident hand on his father's shoulder. Stepping beside Garlic, he announced, "He's been with them all day, joining in their games, and that. You know all the kinds of people who come by for the Alvian market."

"A strange man?" the father questioned, shattering Brandon's entire explanation. Clearly, the father was questioning the innocence of the burly, wrapped outsider.

"Cari," Michael muttered, grabbing the attention of the younger girl. "Please help me. Remember what I did for you and your brother that time you got in trouble?"

Cari puffed her cheeks out, sucked them in, and focused on her father. "He's a friend of theirs."

Brandon's words began to fail him and his father. He remained silent.

"A friend?" Brandon's father questioned.

"Yeah, I met him the other day when Brandon and I went to the market!" Cari stepped forward, trying to ward off the prying caution of her uncle but to no avail as Brenna leaped into the fray, not noticed by the father and son.

"Dad, he's a friend of…," Brenna whipped her head to the first person on her left. "Sandra!"

"Oh?" the old man mused.

If there was one person he'd trust, it was Cassandra, whom he thought of as the intelligent, responsible rich girl who kept them all in mind. The assumption was unfair, but it only played to their strengths in this situation. She took the situation into her control with a demeaning glare at Michael.

Politely, she continued, "Oh, him? He's an actor for a role in the theater. He's trying to stay in his role, however, as it demands the actor to spend the majority of the show looking like *that*. He is trying to get used to it."

Brandon nodded several times in agreement, a little melodramatically. "Yeah, there's a secret performance planned. We're all in on it because of Sandra. Don't tell anyone."

"Eh? A secret show?" the elderly man inquired.

"Yes, a secret… show." Brandon felt a bead of sweat as his father took a step back.

"And they've already cast the roles?" he continued, his skeptical tone gradually replaced by a more joyful, placid one. He seemed distant at best as his interest began to slip.

"Yes…?" Brandon answered, his voice revealing his uncertainty.

He wrinkled his nose and looked at Cassandra. "Oh, have they? Are there any parts left?"

Cassandra bit the inside of her cheek as she thought for a reply. "I… don't know. It is something my father planned."

"Oh, really?" Michael suddenly interjected. Though his snide remark was brushed away, his comment didn't help the situation.

"Anyway, Dad, the metal's going to cripple if you don't get there and sort it out," Brandon joked, patting his father's tense back.

"I think they're going for a theme!" Cari said aloud, much to the shock of everyone. She seemed pleased just to get a word in.

"Ah, well, I applaud your commitment to staying in your role." He turned away. "My boy is right, though. I shouldn't leave the smith unattended. Stay safe, everyone, and it was good to see you all." As he took his leave, Brandon and Cari quickly rushed after him and matched his pace, asking several questions about taking the day off, to which Brandon's father exclaimed, "I already told you that you could!"

Michael spun toward the group. "Another lie, huh?" he whispered to Cassandra, who took the blow and accepted it.

"Michael," Sophia began, stepping in while the rest of the group slowly backed off. "You know what her dad is like. She had to."

"She didn't have to. I thought she stood by us. Instead, we're just some guilty pleasure she escapes to when the high life gets too much…."

"Michael, please," Cassandra muttered, a stubborn look on her face as she gestured toward Brandon's return. His younger cousin followed alongside him, a skip in her step.

"All right, what's going on?" Brandon looked directly at Garlic. "Who is this guy really?"

"And what is the performance as well?" Cari added.

"There is no performance," Michael explained and gestured to Garlic. "And this... *Garlic* is our main problem. We're trying to get him across town to help him. He's really nice and not what we expected."

Brandon got awfully close, to the extent that Scarlett was repulsed enough to want to be put down. "An outlaw?"

"I'm no criminal, not technically," Garlic replied, nonchalant.

"Then I don't want any more lies. Since I did you a favor, you do me one. Who is *this*?" He stared at Michael.

Michael sighed. "A vampire," he mumbled.

"A what?"

"He's a... vampire."

Brandon nodded, slow and steady. "A... what?"

"A... *vampire*," Michael repeated in a whisper.

"Oh...," Brandon slowly turned, and on instinct pulled both Cari and Brenna to his side. His and Garlic's eyes met, and a confrontation of no words began. It was only thought on Brandon's side—the realization that the young man had a choice, and his intuition challenged him to make the right one.

7

"Brenna," Brandon began, his voice coarse as he struggled to come to grips with the current situation. Brenna looked up at her bulky brother, as did the rest of the group. Brandon was the decider between an end to their life-risking game of hide-and-seek and their newest ally in their mission to get Garlic across town.

Much to the group's quiet panic as tensions increased, Brandon now looked back to Garlic and frowned—a bad sign of what was to come. Brandon couldn't find his tongue; his face felt frozen in place. He looked down at Brenna who slipped away from his protective hold. Brandon was further stunned, a glint of worry in his eyes as she went to Garlic's side.

"I trust him," Brenna said peacefully. The group looked at Brandon, who then looked at Michael. Michael merely nodded, confirming his suspicions. Slowly, Brandon looked over his shoulder at his father's smithy that clunked and burned away at raw metal and charcoal alike.

"Brandon, please," Brenna said, using his name with purpose. He felt his heart miss a beat. Fear poured from him, and he wondered if this were really happening, even as people in the background left the market, and a single yell would alert everyone in the local area. Even if it were all true… then what? He didn't know the answer and didn't want to.

"Do you trust him?" His question, purely, was for Brenna, who had already provided her answer. Yet she knew he wanted a settled confirmation.

"I do," she said and looked up at Garlic. "He is nice. I promise."

"Brenna...."

"Please," she near-begged, though whether or not it was for Garlic's protection or for herself was unclear. Garlic felt the tone *slip*. In this moment, he saw a group who were dedicated to helping him. But now, that same group was beginning to realize that Brandon, a close friend of their group, was struggling over whether to help or betray them. And this painted a different picture.

This wasn't just a game. This wasn't a situation in which if Brandon were to just go back to work and not say a word, that'd be that. No, this was a make-or-break situation. Either he was going to have to raise the alarm, or their new ally would feel obligated to give them the last push they needed toward completing their mission.

Brandon looked at the group, now seeing a collection of young people in over their heads—foolish but brave. He respected them, not their choices. And yet, he blamed himself. He could have turned them away, but then what would have happened? His understanding of their peril left him feeling differently. Guilt filled him. This group liked him, at least, so he hoped. Reality was not as kind as them. Reality told them they were all in danger. This moment was a decider above all else.

Garlic looked with stony eyes at Brandon. He felt cold.

The group's quiet begging came from their realization; they knew now more than ever just how messed up their situation was. Or, at least, Garlic hoped they did, for better and for worse.

Brandon sighed, defeated inside. The group's shuffling nearly knocked Garlic into the sun's rays. He swiftly bounced back, though he was hardly subtle about it.

"Okay…, okay. *Okay.* I'm on board. Bring me up to speed," Brandon requested.

"He doesn't want to hurt anyone," Michael explained. "He's kind and honest and genuinely wants to get across town."

"And what is his proof?"

Michael's pupils flared as he looked at Garlic. "What is your proof again?"

Garlic bit his lip and slowly opened his mouth, within which two sharp fangs revealed themselves before he closed his mouth to hide the gleaming, sharp points away. "I mean no harm. You have my word. Once I am safely on the other side of this town, I will simply leave. Nothing more, nothing less."

Brandon nodded. "Look, your teeth looked like anyone's, okay?"

"Well… they have to come out. They only do so on reaction when I'm about to drink." Garlic looked up at the sun's rays. "Okay, look," he said, and for a single, unbearable moment, just enough that it was manageable, he put forth his clothed hand, removed what wrappings and gloves kept him safe, and thrust it forward into the sun.

A single second passed before he shot backward again. He revealed the tinge of smoky, cooked flesh on his hand. "It's slow and painful. It doesn't kill, or at least it hasn't yet but prefers to leave me in suffering rather than death." Garlic slowly wrapped his hand, though the action was clearly a struggle. The group came to his aid, their sympathy provided, and their trust sealed by his willingness to risk pain for them.

"We need to get him more cloth," Cassandra decided, then spun away, half the group rushing with her. Garlic watched them go, and though he wondered how they might wrap him up, he knew there was no harm in nice, clean fabrics. Hopefully with a nice smell.

"Is that evident enough?" Michael asked whilst Cassandra ran back to the market.

Brandon nodded. "I'm sorry. And thank you for… that."

"It was my pleasure." Garlic noticed Brandon's confusion. "If the choice was to be revealed or suffer a moment of pain and not be revealed, I'd rather the latter."

"Understandable... so, you *really* are?"

"Indeed."

Brandon hummed and looked around. His voice, untroubled, asked, "I'm confused. Why have you taken an inside route?"

Garlic opened his mouth to speak—

"Hidden in plain sight," Cassandra answered suddenly.

"Oh, that's good," Brandon commented, and Michael's gently gasped-out noise of displeasure was ignored by all but Brandon—though he seemed confused over it. Tension hung in the air like an omen.

"Then... the best option for us is to keep moving. I'll lead. Let's keep the atmosphere around us casual too. The group is bigger now. So, I need everyone to act more natural and stop crowding around... uh, Garlic. Just move as a loose group but not too loose, with the tallest of us near him. Got it?" The small crowd voiced its approval, and they were on their way with Scarlett's roars of determination to "Save Garlic" among the loudest.

To the average passerby, the group looked like they were simply seeking garlic... for some odd, out-of-place reason. They were a mixed-and-matched group of kids, really, and there was no better time for everyone to pass a blind eye—except for when Garlic began to heave as the group grasped all that they could and draped it over him, some of them even tearing fabric from their clothing to better protect Garlic's skin.

He could barely see by the time they were down the street, and the big blubber of cloth caused him to waddle almost like a penguin. For a moment, he wondered why exactly they felt the need to practically tie up his legs. They found it amusing and spoke little of it. He wanted them to enjoy their time as it only worked in Brandon's favor, portraying them as a "natural, loose group," whatever that was supposed to mean.

Brandon's leadership and direction took them on an unswerving, straightforward path, and though Garlic questioned none of it, he also knew that the young man could still trap and betray him. Even if he had the best intentions, he wondered how he would ever get past the gate and the border guard.

His hope rested more in Cassandra, who was meek and distant and not as he had hoped she would be. She was his best bet, he felt, but she currently took to the sidelines due to internal drama. Michael was not much help either. To see his two biggest advantages divided to the point that they now served no purpose caused him fear, and potentially grief, should things go wrong.

A girl from a rich family lies to her overly judgmental, protective parents as to what she does during the day. He cast a glance toward her white, muddied dress and how it now seemed the least of her worries. She picked at it, nonetheless. *I understand, truly… but lies always surface in the end. Honesty got me this far.* He smiled to himself. *To an extent.*

His hope, then, was on what questions they would continue to ask. He felt that tension rise among the group, and the longer it remained, the higher the chance one of them might *snap* under the pressure and choose to betray him out of fear of what would be done to them otherwise.

Time went onward, and for once, as Brandon sidled close to him, he knew what was coming and beat him to it this time.

"Why did you help me?"

8

"Huh?" Brandon turned to Garlic.

"You are under no obligation to help me. So, why did you?" He wanted nothing more than to understand why exactly the young man chose to assist him.

The question had been sitting in the far reaches of his mind for the most part, but now, it surfaced as something so much more. It was an odd situation, certainly, with a very strange group.

Whilst Brandon took his time to think, he studied Michael, a young man in his own right who stood ready near his side, a step or two behind. Michael ventured outward into the beyond of what, in his mind, may as well have been paradise. Garlic knew the young man came from a lesser neighborhood, and that was putting it kindly. Regardless, he was torn mentally and was of no help now, offering nothing more than a worried glance sideways from time to time.

Then, there was Cassandra with her white, muddied, flowing dress. Against the sun, her slightly pale skin looked hot and flustered, her ginger hair still tied up in a bun as when they first met.

Their eyes met, and awkwardness passed between them. He knew from her blue eyes, the glint they held, that when she had swiftly changed her view to Michael that the person really on her mind wasn't the vampire. He appreciated that, in a way, the teenage drama seemed to not be taking precedence over the fact that an immortal, mean, keen, killing machine was right there. Literally, in the center of their formation, waddling like a fat duck made of cloth, was that killing machine, with his horde of ducklings following after him.

She turned away. The last he saw was the way every last freckle on her face moved with the saddened drooping of her features. The two were tense, but Garlic had been alive long enough to know when something more lurked in the hearts of humanity.

When Brandon apologized for not knowing how to answer his question, Garlic minded little. At that moment, Luke, the young boy with tussled black hair, begrimed clothes, and a petite bit of chub to his cheeks reminded Garlic how playful the group could be. Especially when he was handed another piece of cloth.

"What am I to do with this, child?" Garlic asked, curious.

"I don't know where else to wrap you up...," Luke looked behind them, walking backward for a moment. "Most of it keeps falling off. Christopher, keep picking it up!"

"On it!" yelled back Christopher, the teen who was rough in voice and older than Luke by a few years at most. He was fairly tall, and his brown eyes, brown hair, brown tunic, and brown everything else made Garlic fear if the teen ripped anymore of his fabric off, there would be nothing left to shelter himself with.

"You aren't thinking straight," Andrew, the blond, messy teen, said, a grin plastered across his face. "You're forgetting his face!"

"I need to be able to see," Garlic reminded him, only for Christopher to hand Andrew a pile of fallen cloth. Andrew passed it to Luke, who then had it stolen by Sophia, the young teen whom he first met and wished inside that she'd kept quiet and run along.

"He needs to be able to see!" yelled Sophia at her brother.

"Thank you," Garlic muttered, grateful that she had a sense of reason.

"He has us to guide him, you pig-headed fool!" Andrew argued back, playful more so than argumentative.

Sophia gasped and threw the pile of cloth in her hands at Brandon. She didn't back down, and while Andrew ran, gleeful that he had successfully wound her up, it didn't stop her from chasing him. His comment led to them having the most sportive of brawls.

Andrew and Sophia continued hurling insults, Garlic turned to Brandon, who was lagging behind a little. He scrambled to pick up all the cloth.

Brandon finally caught up and grumbled as the cloth wrapping came to an end. He stared at the pile of fabric and turned to Garlic.

"Don't look at me. I can hardly waddle."

Brandon nodded and turned to Scarlett, who had been holding Brenna's hand. They walked as close to Garlic as possible. "Scarlett, would you like to hold this?" Brandon asked.

Scarlett looked up, curious. Brenna, however, was terrified. "She'll be smothered."

"She'll be fine," Brandon reassured her.

"She'll drown in all that," Brenna protested.

"She'll be fine."

"She'll probably die."

"She'll be *fine*."

"I'll be *fine*," Scarlett repeated and sprung upward, both of her hands shooting in his direction. Brandon peered down at the tiny Scarlett as did Brenna and Garlic.

"I don't think she'll be fine," Emma quietly intervened.

Scarlett huffed, and in her protest, wandered over to Michael in the hopes he might do something, only to receive light laughs and cottony words for her trouble.

Garlic smiled at the childish nature of Scarlett and passed a glance to Brenna in her hunter's garb, again wondering why she had gone so far out of her way to surpass the safe area they used for their typical games of hide-and-seek. He was impressed by her lack of fear and curiosity.

"Uh, Abby, could you hold this for me?" Brandon finally inquired as Brenna rejected him. Abby, the quiet, carefree teenager, looked as if she hadn't a clue what was happening as she plodded along near the front of the group.

How old is she? Garlic pondered, confused by her appearance and demeanor. He had forgotten she was even among them. *She's so small. But… she must be fifteen? Sixteen, maybe?*

She gave a hum, which confused Brandon, and then a shrill whistle. He concluded that it meant "yes." One swift move later, and in her arms was a pile of cloth. She questioned nothing of it.

Does she know I'm an immortal being? He met her eye, and she smiled. *Maybe. Is she aware of what is going on?*

The smooth, clean voice of Brandon murmured, "What was your question again?"

"Ah, it was… why? Why have you and…?" Garlic looked at the smaller, intelligent girl nearby.

"That's Cari. Would you believe she is only a year older than Scarlett?"

"She's…. Well, that's interesting." Garlic met her eye, and she smiled, and for a moment, they shared the other's pain as he wore an insurmountable amount of mismatched clothing and she wore clothing one size too large. She didn't know his discomfort, but she gave her understanding, nonetheless.

"Scarlett is only eight. Somehow, so childish at heart. Probably because Michael's so serious. Someone's got to keep things lively." Freeing was the joke at Michael's expense, and the shared laughter that came lifted the tension off his shoulders, even if only for a moment—until Cassandra gave a small giggle, and it all came crashing back down. At last, Brandon noticed and moved quickly to advance the conversation elsewhere. Garlic understood that the young man had only just realized the tension between them.

"I helped you because of the circumstances. I trust Michael and Sandra and my sister." Brandon's voice, low, and stern, spoke honestly. "I'll be frank, Garlic, I don't like this at all. However, I'm not my mother, and her sacred hate of your kind made me grow up with a want to know the other side of the story, you see?"

"Well, my kind is no kind. I am one, and I am cursed."

Brandon blinked. "Not born?"

"No, though most tend to assume there are several apical families and some scheme around it… I refuse to talk about it. I am truly just one, and alone, created by the real dangers of this world that no one cares to look at until it is too late. I am used to being the monster when there is far worse out there." Garlic heaved out a heavy breath, a weight on his chest. "I'm being too open."

"No, no, it's okay. It's good you're honest. Puts me at ease with putting my neck on the line like this. I don't think a lot of these kids realize how dangerous this is. Learning about you, and just... talking makes it easier. Makes me like you. Makes me think you're not *so* bad." For once, Garlic was overjoyed inside to know at least one of them was wise enough to realize how dangerous the situation and their actions were. "Look, we don't care overall. My father always liked tales of mystical creatures. Mother hated them, though."

"I imagine if your mother was present, I'd be out of luck."

"Likely, yes." Brandon chuckled to himself. "She would throw commonplace water at you and scream that it is holy."

Garlic winced. "Well, is it blessed?"

Brandon looked at him. "Uh, why does it matter?"

Garlic, appalled, was left horrified on the inside. He struggled to show it on the outside, though, as his waddles and nearly fully covered face gave him no leeway to express himself. "It's all fun and games until it is actually holy water, young man."

Brandon, confused, laughed it off as he questioned his entire existence. It was a look Garlic knew all too well. "Look, um... well, I have another question for you."

"It'd be my pleasure to answer another question, though…." A subject lingered on Garlic's mind—one that he wondered would be better left unsaid. "May I ask you a question first?"

"May as well."

Garlic licked his lips, though it didn't save him from the bitter taste in his mouth. "I've been alive long enough to see all corners of history… and I've visited this place on more than one occasion. Not this town specifically as it didn't exist before the fourteenth century." Garlic sighed. "I think I'll get to the point. You're a young man whose appearance is uncanny to see in an area such as this." Garlic flashed a gesture at his arm. Brandon's confusion was fair, though he understood a moment after. It was something he was aware of. "I only mean my question on a social level, I suppose. I've been alive for a long time, and there has been great change, so much so that I cannot keep up with all the several corners of this globe… or so on."

Brandon offered a faint smile. "I understand," he said and presented the color of his skin. "What you're asking is how I came to live here despite… recent times?"

"Exactly." Garlic looked at him, earnest and sincere. He meant nothing, and Brandon saw as much from the vampire. He was immortal, after all—what hadn't he seen? It was a thought Brandon pondered and knew needed no answer.

"See," Garlic began again, "a couple hundred years ago, it would have been incredibly rare or even unheard of to see a man such as yourself in a place like this. The circumstances are new to me. I hope to learn of why this change has occurred."

Brandon laughed a hearty laugh indeed. The group was caught up in their own chatter as the eternal being who walked among them spoke of how society had begun to shift, something that Brandon now went into a great freeze about. He had no clue as to how to answer. Garlic saw that. It was as if he were transparent in his emotions. Brandon had no word or idea of where to begin.

"Your family," Garlic began. "By what means did your family receive this life?"

"*Receive?*" Brandon near-muttered. "Well…," he looked Garlic dead in the eye. "It's the life I know, I guess. Something I've considered but not questioned. My father tells me stories of his grandfather. See, he fought during the 'US War of Independence,'" Brandon thought hard, biting the inside of his cheek as he did so. "My great-grandfather was a slave there and was offered a chance of freedom should he fight for the British. He took that chance, fought hard, and got it."

"They kept their deal?"

"Somewhat."

Garlic nearly cooed at the prospect of such a change in the times. "It is so interesting... I adore these new changes. I hope to see it improve with time."

"Eh? Oh. Uh, yes, me too. Like I said, it's life to me, here. I can thank my ancestor for that. My grandfather passed recently.... If you'd spoken to him, he might've given you a greater idea of their transition across the sea to, well, here." Brandon looked to the sky. It hadn't seemed so long ago that the morning had become afternoon, and now it was mere hours away from evening. "It's a cold time of year.... Night'll be on us soon."

"That it will." Garlic said nothing more. He took the hint in his stride to let the conversation slip.

"I'm sorry. Nevertheless, thank you. The past one hundred years alone have changed rapidly compared to the more ancient history I've lived through. So many people now...."

Brandon gave a low laugh.

Moving the subject along, I see. Garlic felt happy, at least, that he wasn't involved with the nervous group's bickering or the tension between Cassandra and Michael. He felt that his being there was causing their friction to grow, and a burden rested on his shoulders as a result.

"Are you some awe-inspiring, legendary fighter?"

Garlic snorted. "A what?"

"Well, you are… *you know*…. So, you must be a warrior, right?" Brandon looked at him with hope and nervousness. Social anxiety was a fair thing to feel when talking to a waddling vampire who could hardly see.

Garlic shook his head, amused. "I'm what I am, but I am not an incredible warrior. Everything I have learned over my eternity of life comes from pure survival instinct. In a fight, I've learned to run. If I have to kill, I'll hunt. I don't desire the fight."

"You'll hunt?" Brandon questioned.

"Indeed. I'll never fight outrightly unless I am backed into a corner. I've been alive for a long time and had to learn from experience and humanity the same way everyone else does in the game of survival."

"So, you are a hunter, not a fighter?"

"Exactly."

Brandon's lips pulled backward, then upward. His face lit up, almost. "That's actually… enlightening. You don't like the fight, but you will hunt."

Garlic died inside. He knew where this was going. "It is an animal instinct. Like you, I must survive, and bodily needs must be attended to."

Brandon, confident now, asked bluntly, "Hunger?"

"Yes."

"Water?"

"I drink the same as any other."

Brandon nodded, excited somewhat. "I'm confused, but this is interesting."

Garlic's face flashed with surprise. He was used to the curiosity of those willing to listen, and honestly, it never ceased to amaze him either. The ratio of those who wanted him dead compared to those who wanted to learn more about him was far too balanced for his liking. Recent centuries, in his opinion, had shown some form of change taking place.

"You're inquisitive?" Garlic asked.

"Ah, yeah…," Brandon raised an eyebrow, his mind left to rot away as he couldn't decipher the word at play, yet it was so familiar. He swore it. He swore he knew it. No, it couldn't be what he thought it was. Or what it might mean. He didn't know. But he felt he did. He hated that it was now, in this very moment of all times, that his mind had to crash and burn while talking with what was the most important figure life had to offer him right now. This was just terrible.

"It means you're very curious," Cassandra said to cut the awkward silence.

"Thank you," Brandon muttered.

"What else do you know?" Michael's inquiry to Cassandra was… offbeat. It felt unneeded and out of place. Everyone heard. No one really understood it, and thus, everyone turned away and went back to their business. Ignorance on the part of the group only left a greater toll on Garlic, adding to his guilt. The two teens were proceeding from tension to brusque, passive-aggressive comments. Cassandra said nothing else of it.

Garlic turned back to Brandon. *As long as I convince him, I shall be fine. You are my new hope now, young man.*

"Well, know this: Regardless of my curse, and what I think and feel about the world, life is precious, and to me, it is just as much so because of how long I'll live. Yet, more often than not, life isn't precious because it is life. It is what that life does.... I'm a bit twisted and believe my view can be chaotic. Honestly... I admit it depends on the question."

Brandon, slightly lost, spoke fairly. "And... at the moment, you are feeling...?"

"Incredibly happy to know a young group such as yourselves aren't judging or betraying me. You'd be surprised how hard such company is to come by."

9

Commoners turned to elegant women in frilly dresses and an overabundance of facial makeup alongside men who stood tall and proud, suited, and more; the picture was already painted of a quainter, thinner population among the wealthier side of town.

It wasn't all set in stone, and there were some variations in the fashion of the people around. Some wore far more casual clothing, but it didn't stop their posh attitude at times, based on how they were interacting with nearby merchants and market stalls.

His expectation of the stereotype of the rich was broken several times over. It didn't mean that they weren't more cautious overall. The citizenry was guarded and judgmental of the group yet still happy to mind their business and go about their day. It provided an opportunity in a way for the group.

Their journey took them through open areas, wider streets, past horses and carriages, across grand architecture and reverence-garnering houses. The stone-paved roads, gravelly in texture, had stone dust that crunched under their shoes.

The restaurants, taverns, and inns boasted fine smells and mouth-watering foods. The group was often distracted by their discussions about favorite meals, foods, and the finer cuisines that life had to offer.

Garlic all the while felt it best not to tell them that if he were hungry and had to pick, Sophia would probably be his choice to drink. Her blood and scent were somewhat alluring. He wondered if that was why he had been caught in the first place. He felt if she were alone, he might have taken the chance. But she was only a teen, and he had a job to do. If it weren't for the agreements he had made with underground societies, unknown from the common populace, he knew he'd be more feral now, like he was in the ancient days. Now, he had a target elsewhere, one that would be a feast and quell his thirst. He just needed patience—something he reminded himself of constantly.

No, enough of that. I am above this. I am more than base instinct. Garlic held his head high. *Focus… somewhere else.* He looked at the buildings. *I wonder what the Romans would've thought of this architecture.* He frowned. *I like Georgian Architecture… but… an eternity of change also leaves me biased. I've seen some incredible things in my lifetime. Ah, what I would do to see the pyramids being built again! It is still a wonder how they ever pulled it off to begin with. I don't think I'll ever quite understand.*

Nostalgia washed over the immortal. He took his mind away from the scent of blood at last. He felt this was a lovely place, a lovely town, yet he had already forgotten the name of it. Traveling the world several times over often made it difficult to keep it all in mind. Or, at least, that was how he felt.

With each passing second, he noticed the group's tension lessening. Now that they were calmer, they seemed more carefree. The task of wrapping him up with more cloth was over for good.

He looked at them all, unsure whether they could protect him. The sun could kill him, and they took every precaution to avoid him falling beneath its rays. Their formation was strong, but it appeared lackluster. With the group's carefree attitude also came a looser formation.

Outsiders saw an odd group that was just parading through the town for fun—or, at least, that was how it looked on the surface. No one knew of the vampire they harbored at the center of their group.

The hot day around them slipped away. It had been no more than a few hours at the most, perhaps less, and yet, winter's bite was a reminder of the sun's dying presence. What they saw and felt now were its last legs. To Cassandra, it was all the more reason to rush Garlic through the town—night wasn't far away. Evening fast approached.

The bitter cold settled in, gradual at first but more quickly as the day dragged on. The sun now hovered above them as the day neared its end. The potential shadows were lessening and the paths available to the group were disappearing. Their options changed with time, as did their route, making the journey longer than expected.

Though the detour was needed, the group wasn't any livelier because of it. With a long day behind them, they were tired, sweaty, and glummer than they were before.

Cassandra whipped her head from side to side, hands fiddling with the tight bun it was in before, at last, she set it free, the clump of hair gracefully falling down into a wave of beautiful ginger hair, wavy and curled in its style.

Often enough, when the bickering ended, they all found themselves focused on the same potent issue: there was a vampire in their midst. Sooner or later, one of them had to say something about it. He knew they would. It was too uncanny and suspicious, and he imagined some of them questioned the legitimacy of his claim.

What more can I do or say to make you believe me? His thoughts went unanswered, and he tried to think nothing more of it. He could not have asked for more from their group, and it was certainly not the first time in his long history of being alive that he had found himself having to rely upon a group of kind, open-minded people to help get from point A to point B. Often enough in his history, had time told of the death or suffering of others based on their association with him.

He focused elsewhere. *The roads are smooth,* he thought, *and maintained.* Everything about it was grand to all but Cassandra and, after a time, Garlic.

How much longer could they go on? He didn't know. How much longer could they remain undetected? He wished he had the answer.

Now more than ever seemed a good time to sneak around the outside, as the guards present were more numerous and highly trained too. He looked upon them often and felt a knot in his gut over the knowledge that, based on the way their group operated, even with Cassandra trying to take the helm as she was often recognized by the townsfolk, this could not last.

The group was too open and easy to spot; curious eyes were already beginning to question what such a large, mixed group was trying to accomplish as they marched in a singular direction. It was too clear now where they wanted to go. The furthest border gate may as well have been in view.

"We need to talk again," Garlic said to the group, his voice low and rough, not as a way to urge them onward but to remind them of the stakes involved. He wasn't sure of what to talk about. "Michael?" he prompted.

Michael provided nothing but a disconnected stare.

"Do you have to play with your food?" asked a familiar voice.

Garlic spun, baffled. "Where are you, little child?"

"Little?" He found Andrew once again at his side.

"Sorry?" Garlic said as the smaller-than-average teenager marched alongside him.

"Do you smear blood everywhere and tear them open? Spraying blood and... taking their entrails and stuff?"

Horrified. He was horrified. Garlic's mouth near enough hung open. "Boy, what exactly goes on inside your head?"

Andrew seemed gladdened. "My father says that a lot too." Just as abruptly as he had shown so much cheer, he saddened. "*A lot.*"

Garlic recoiled. "Well, not a lot shocks me, though that was backlash-worthy."

Andrew ran his fingers through his blond locks and looked up at him. "Yeah?"

Garlic forced a small smile as Abby nearly tripped over all the fabric she was holding. It had drooped down in places where longer threads began to slip.

"Do you believe me to be a savage?" Garlic asked.

Andrew looked at him as if he had seen something truly horrible, something utterly inconceivable, something so out of this world that all he could manage to utter was, "No, that's why I was asking."

He's just truly curious? Garlic nodded. "I assume you like the thrill of the battle and the fight and the monster side of things? Well, I'll tell you this...,"

Garlic quieted his voice. "The hunt for a human is the same as the hunt for a man or woman to an animal. Once it is done, it also serves a purpose. I'm not some mindless creature. I get hungry, I hunt. I kill." He watched as the young teen's face filled with merriment.

"That's incredible."

Garlic ignored his excitement. "I eat… or better put, drink. I'm no different from the man who hunts an animal into extinction, and most likely, that man might be glory-hunting."

I hope I can find a way to remind him that what he might find interesting, is also a curse to me.

"Speaking of that," Brandon interjected, "my father is hugely upset with the whole glory-hunting business. He thinks it is worthless."

Brandon's words didn't go unmissed as the group all agreed in their arrays of ways, whether it be hums, nods, or the like.

"I assume you… uh, Garlic, don't like it? The glory-hunting?" Andrew asked, twiddling his fingers.

Garlic wished he could provide more emotion, but he physically couldn't. "In my eyes, the man is morally wrong, whilst I, the vampire, am nothing more than an animal in its prime looking to survive."

A second of understanding passed. "That's *impressive*," Andrew decided, thrilled at the delightful conversation they had, whilst everyone who over-heard rebounded in horror at Andrew's asking and the answers that were given.

Garlic raised his eyebrows in a way he had never done before. Well, on second thought, maybe he had. He had been alive for quite some time. "Is it, though?"

"It seems you're, like, a polite hunter?"

Garlic fumbled for his words. "You're… not… wrong. I'll never make a mess. Food is food, and I don't know how many humans will gladly make a mess of what they eat. I'm not a fool, and smeared blood, torn wounds, and more are worthless." Garlic looked at the group, who looked back at him quietly. "If you don't believe me, think about it."

Scarlett whispered, "I don't get it."

He smiled warmly. "Why would I waste…," he whispered, "…*blood*?"

The group's echoes of "ooh" and "oh" stirred quite the pandemonium of bickering.

Andrew shot back at him, "Wait. If that's true, how do you hunt someone?"

Garlic shoved back what his senses screamed at him of danger and kept himself steady and blissfully ignorant. If he looked like he didn't want to be caught, he'd be caught. Or, at least, he tried to think of the best explanation to use if he did get caught.

Being caught isn't the issue, as much as I don't want to be. It is the mess I'll create if I am that's the problem. They, the town, can try to catch me, but they'll fail like the rest of history has before them. These children don't understand, do they? I'm a vampire. I'm akin to a lost animal who can speak.

"I prefer to break my opponent. Crack bones, maybe? Or just snap the neck—the easiest option. Any blood spilled is a waste in my eyes... and messy."

Andrew went through various stages of excitement, awe, confusion, fear, and finally, wonder.

Cassandra asked about the phrase Garlic had rummaged about in his mind. "What do you mean by *opponent?*"

"You two," Michael interjected and sidled close enough to separate them. "As amazing and disturbing as it is to discern the fact from the fiction, your topic isn't exactly safe." Michael nudged away Andrew, who fought back long enough for Chris and Luke to tug him away from the vampire. The group realized how open and lively they were and that the comments made were likely jokes or something of the sort. Still, it didn't help how odd the man of fabric at their center was.

The group noticed a looming danger as the guards began to follow. '

10

Garlic hadn't noticed.

The group noticed.

People on the sidelines noticed them.

One woman whispered, much to the displeasure of Garlic's ears, *"Did he say he cracks bones...?"*

"Whose bones?" her companion queried.

"I don't know."

"What are they doing?" another distant voice wondered.

"Where are they going?" yet another chimed in curiously.

Andrew looked guilty.

Garlic hated it—how the children felt responsible for simply being open and outgoing. He hated relying on the children, hated what might happen to them should he be caught or ousted, if not for being a vampire than as someone who obviously looked at least criminal-worthy.

They only follow, nothing more.

The quietness that took every one of them was disturbing, to say the least. They knew what might come or what probably would.

Michael sighed. "Garlic, I'm not in the best of moods... and I'm sorry for that, but...," his voice fell to a hushed warning. "Look, Garlic, it might be best to be quiet, for now. I don't mean any offense to ya."

Garlic shook his head. "Each interaction is as interesting as the last. I don't often get to speak to the next youngest generation, you see." Garlic peered to the sky and felt happy to be caught in the shade of a building's roof. "And I've seen a lot of them."

Michael murmured something under his breath, and then, louder, repeated, "Uh, how is this generation?"

Garlic looked among their group and saw nothing but joy from all of them. He felt pride and trust in them. "Good, thus far, based on how open-minded you all are."

Michael, flustered, shoved his hands into his raggedy pockets. "Well… thank you." Michael spared a quick look at Cassandra, and for a second, his eyes showed nothing but hurt… *and want.* "You've been alive for a long time, right?"

Garlic replied, plain in tone and expression, "Immortal."

Michael nodded, unsure. His hands fiddled with his lower garments before he shoved them into his pockets. Among the stir of the group, Michael was the one to ponder something unique. They walked and walked, and all the while, the group asked questions. He assumed they were questions the vampire had received time and time again.

We're probably not the first to share words with you, Michael thought. *But, if I never see you again, then…?* He trod on a pebble and cursed the sudden ache in his foot. *If I am going to ask an immortal person something grand and important… now is the time.*

"Do you have… any advice?"

Garlic's hobbled walk had a skip to it after that question. The group turned a corner, avoiding a patrol on the route they hoped to take. Brandon and Cassandra worked as one to lead the group on the rightful path. Michael stood in formation, stuck to the side of Garlic as if they were butter and bread.

A sharp gasp expelled from the vampire's chapped lips, and after it, he murmured, "Ah… where do I begin?" Garlic, at peace, thought hard, searching for some kind of unbreakable, useful, mind-shattering advice he could give that would change the young man's life forever.

"About… love," Michael specified.

"*Ah.*"

Michael panicked. He rambled on, "Don't concern yourself with that, please."

"Alas… you asked me."

Michael's voice became agitated and panicky. "We don't have to talk about it."

Garlic looked at Cassandra, then at Michael, then back at Cassandra. His expression made his point clear enough.

"You want to talk about it?" Garlic pressed.

"It's awkward enough that I asked," he said under his breath as they turned another corner. Brandon and

Cassandra navigated the group through crossroads and long streets, around corners and down alleys.

"Michael, is it?" Garlic inquired, and the young man flipped his head to him. "It is."

"Sorry?"

Garlic laughed at the young man's expense. "Oh, how love always finds a way to be admirable and worrying all at once." He laughed again, genuinely, a gorgeous, light laugh, soft overall. His laugh not only left the group in a whirl of hysteria, but even a few locals gave notice to the soft, beautiful echo of the strange man's laughter. It was crisp, clear, and gentle, yet held a cheerful tone. The charisma alone that exuded from his laugh did not go unnoticed, and the group worked hard to keep him pushed into the shade.

Hmm... why should I feel as if I care for the fool's romantic interest? I have suffered as a result of love many times before.... Garlic shot Michael a stare, which did not go unnoticed. *Though I am sapped from past drama and intrigue in my life... perhaps it wouldn't hurt to steer them onto the right path. At least, if not for sheer amusement, I could do so as my way of thanking them both.*

Garlic focused on the route ahead; he appreciated Brandon and Cassandra's work to keep them on shaded routes. He took his hesitation as a chance to think about the question, about what advice to give.

The group around him was distracting. Whilst he was in his conversation with Michael, the group had taken to pondering whether or not Garlic would make a good opera singer or something along those lines. The topic came and went, and he felt nothing but gratitude to their kind words about his voice.

Ahead of him, he saw where Cassandra and Brandon were working hard to plan a route for them to take. The group slowed often, and they were forced to stall while the next shaded path was taken. Still, it didn't mean that the sun was blaring. It was still light outside, but the sun's grasp on their world was beginning to fade.

As much as he appreciated their actions, a part of him felt a strange relief in how long this journey across the town was taking. With every passing minute under the sun, the moon began to rise a little more. They were approaching the last few hours of sunlight, and soon, he would be in his domain. The darkness was his world and where he thrived.

He stared at Cassandra. *I suppose I am the reason they've fallen on the path that they have today. If it weren't for me, they'd have continued to live a lie. Or, at least, she would have.* Garlic pursed his lips and hummed thoughtfully. *Why do I care?*

Cassandra was intelligent, sweet, and well-spoken. She had her demons, but it didn't mean she wasn't constantly thinking of others.

I avoid love… but it doesn't mean I don't enjoy watching it bloom for others. It's not my business, but…. He looked between them both, Michael and

Cassandra, who stayed so close yet so far apart. *An eternal being's fair words won't be harmful.*

He questioned his reasoning for a single moment and shrugged away some petty notions that came to mind, such as, *I'm only doing this in part because I lack any kind of drama in my life.* He avoided the thought, of course. Failure after failure, heartache after heartache…. He knew better. And yet, he turned to Michael at last. *So be it… I hope he'll listen.*

"Young man," Garlic began with a soft voice, "earlier, you spoke a fair question. May I provide some thoughts?"

"Garlic, please. You don't have to. Unless you are going to give me tales of how a vampire has a fulfilling love life?"

"I would rather not speak of me, please. I've lived a long life. Time takes all in the end. Love is a permanent scar that comes from a temporary emotion. It has been far too long since I dared take that route again. I'm sorry, but my past and business are my own, child."

"Okay, I've been listening," Luke said, intervening. "Surely life is worthless without love," his protest was heard and fair. "My parents say love is all."

"Yeah, everyone deserves happiness," Chris added.

"Even… vampires," Abby whispered, nearby.

"I… agree, even through its difficulties, I imagine," Michael said, his eyes on Cassandra, who spoke with Brandon at the front of the group. Garlic saw the look, the reflection of his emotions in his eyes and knew he held hopes she might not know.

"Michael," Garlic said, "I've seen many a tragedy in my time. All of you, hear me too. You speak such things because you may have it differently. I am not human, and I sense the weakness of my prey. I can sense emotions, mortal. If your heart blooms for someone, say it when ready, but never wait forever. Time will not wait for you, as it has for me, and that is not a good thing."

Garlic paused to think of what to say next, though the sudden, strange warmth on his cheek and then the glare in his eyes, which ended with a blazing *agony* he remembered all too well, cut him off entirely from speaking. Wincing, he was cut short by a gleam of sunlight that struck his face.

He shot backward, flinching.

The shade broke just long enough for a slight sizzle to erupt on his left cheek. Thrust backward, Michael knocked him into the shade. He pushed Luke and Chris to the floor in the process as a gentle flow of steam arose from his new, gentle, slow burn.

The panic he'd incited caused fresh eyes to turn to them. Most assumed a fight happened, with one panicked, older teen having knocked down two others, with a strange third being forced into a wall.

The group panicked to help and shroud them, and all Garlic could wonder was how they didn't understand.

They should fear him like any other human, yet they didn't. They felt the terror he gave off, whereas the horror often rested in the local folk and their neighbors. He'd seen it enough. Humanity's darkness was something that most were able to acknowledge but did nothing about.

He wondered how they would feel if they focused on the matter of human blood. It had been, and always would be, his only true source of life. There was no getting around it. A friendly few had even tried to offer him alternatives, but nothing ever worked. He wished there was another way.

Somehow, his mind was able to contemplate these things whilst chaos erupted around them.

In the end, human blood was what he needed to survive. More often than not, a body a month did brilliantly to cover the bare minimum of his needs. Twelve bodies a year for eternity, however, built up some truly wondrous and terrifying numbers.

Patrol guards had watched and followed with weary eyes and itchy fingers. Now, they were spurred into action. They sprinted toward the group and used the bedlam caused by the sunlight to confront them.

They grabbed and pulled at all of them, moving them aside to find the source of the ruckus the group had caused. Anyone in the area knew that the guards only wanted to figure out what they are up to.

A mass of bodies began to crowd the area. Children yelled and teenagers shouted as the guards seized their chance to ambush the children. The guards yelled for more guards. Patrols flooded into the group. It happened quickly as the youngest were neatly arranged on one side whilst the oldest struggled to figure out what was happening. Chris and Luke were pulled up from the floor whilst Michael was forced to his knees.

The guards turned to Garlic.

He stood there, back to the dusty wall, and watched as they began their nervous advance on the most unique member of the group—him.

11

Garlic hoped there and then that the group would betray him. After all, if he was allowed to live, he'd soon have to hunt again.

He hoped he could explain the deals he had made with the dangerous people, deals meant to make his life not a game of cat and mouse, but rather, employment with the benefit of blood at the end of it.

He didn't feel he was a good person. He didn't feel anything. All he saw was how much he understood the reason why the group didn't betray him. They had taken the time to trust him and learn about him, things that he found beyond disturbing considering only a few hours had passed since they met. Yet, this wasn't the first time that had happened. People were often stupid or ignorant, but also sometimes open and curious. This group was the latter.

Then, there was the rest.

He despised the darkness of humanity and yet was happy to nestle in it. He thought how, even if they were to betray him, to tattle on his tales, that they would never achieve anything other than unrest in the town. They forgot who he was: an animal who can feel the adrenaline of survival, of fight or flight, just as much as them.

Was this the time to fight? He looked at them and wondered if this was goodbye as a guard clutched at his thick, clothed arm. Everything was a blur as his left eye was hampered by the destruction that the sun's rays had caused. It was a cloudy day, too, but that didn't change how damaging the sun could be.

He fought back against the rough tugs of the guards. They wanted him exposed, away from the wall and in the light.

Unrelenting, he stood his ground, his muscles tensed and bulging beneath his overload of clothing. When the guard with all his strength could not move him, he released him and backed away in confusion. Still, others tried, and he wished they had left him in the shade.

He hoped as the clear, firm, demanding voice of Cassandra's father rattled through his skull, that whatever trial they gave him would at least be in the shade the wall provided.

He preferred to focus on his pastime—his love for architecture. Oh, how it had changed and developed. How he saw the wealth of top-class Georgian architecture. He loved every last part of what he saw. The openness of the area, a central, open square of sorts, paved and smooth, was surrounded by urban buildings. The rich lived here, and they looked at the reckless group with annoyance and fear. The area only made the circumstances worse.

For a moment, he hated what the architecture represented.

Still, he was hopeful for the new generation who may grow old with a wise kindness to them, not afraid of the world and intelligent enough not to be taken by it either.

I'm overthinking everything. He caught the eye of her father again. It was a brief exchange, but the coldness that passed between them was as sharp as the daggers the guards were told not to draw on the children. It wasn't a steel blade that worried him.

For thousands of years, I've dealt with all types of weaponry, but that.... He looked at the flintlock pistol Cassandra's father had—the man's hand danced around the tip of its holster of hard, thick leather....

Scarlett screamed, and the rest protested alongside her.

Garlic was dragged across the stone pavement and wrestled to and fro; he kept his head down.

Do I act out?

Cassandra's father walked closer, moving like a wave of dread.

It would be quick. Instant.

He clenched his muscles. Standing firm, he became unmovable, the guard's efforts rendered worthless as his instincts kicked in.

This was different, now. Before, he had simply remained firm and unmoving. Now, the feral part of his mind reminded him why he was still alive. He was a monster at the end of the day and would continue to be so. He was an animal at his core and survived like any other. To fall here was not his plan.

He felt his fangs quiver, his hands clench, his body prepare. Blood was going to be spilled no matter what. He was ready.

"Please," Cassandra begged shrilly.

Garlic saw her being held back by a single guard who didn't dare stop her from flailing against him. She broke free and dashed forward like a frightened horse. Her father was near, and he looked down like a bear might at its prey.

Garlic shrugged off the guards. No more resistance came his way. He was a big, blubbery-looking fool covered in cloth, though underneath was a hardened, honed warrior. He didn't consider himself a fighter, but he could become one when needed.

And he would.

"Father!"

Her voice… so afraid. So… scared?

She was determined to stop him. She wouldn't let things end as they were about to. Brandon fought against the guards, and when he did, Michael, who was on his knees, tried to in his own right.

Garlic saw the group, full of young adults, teenagers, and children.

I can lash out. I can survive.

Scarlett looked at him with red, puffy eyes. If anything, she seemed confused and lost. He saw a little girl who would soon know the truth of what he was.

A little girl who might just grow up with a view different than the others. Being the youngest, he knew the scars he could inflict on her mentally would cut the deepest—such lacerations into the mind could ruin a soul several times over.

Everything around him faded at that moment as she spun away from his view. He wasn't sure if she had moved or was moved or if he had stumbled or simply looked away. He felt a guilt in his heart for actions he hadn't committed to.

Do I truly care for them? He began to focus. He growled, a seething curse slipped through his lips, but the words went unheard.

The chaos went quiet in his ears. It was but a gentle ringing, like a distant bell.

What lesson could I possibly teach the new generation? They would only come to fear me and assume what they were taught was right. Garlic turned to Cassandra. *Save me, please.*

Cassandra leaped at him, not her father, outmaneuvering him and placing herself between himself and the man with the steel-filled stare.

At last, he prepared to draw his flintlock pistol.

And her, now standing before him, left him frozen.

It shouldn't have been a difficult situation. Yet her father was clearly conflicted over two thoughts. One remembered she was his flesh and blood; the other reminded him that duty called.

"You have no right nor reason to hurt or imprison this man. He has every right to be here as you do. If you'd just listen…!" Her shout left a worse silence.

She looked over her shoulder. With quick steps, she forced Garlic backward until he was returned into the shade and against the wall. Gentle arrays of wavy steam still arose from his cheek, the sizzling reminiscent of the sound of bacon upon a fire. He was in agony.

He bit down hard, teeth gritted, and placed his trust in her. It was a two-way situation. He realized then, even as the soldiers removed everyone else from the swarm around Garlic, that Cassandra was his only hope. No one dared lay a hand on her because of her father.

He stood there, still and silent like a disgruntled slab of upright rock.

Strung on the girl's father's hip sat the iron and bronze of his flintlock pistol, filled with gunpowder and ready to be fired. His hand danced there, though, uncertain.

"Father, please—"

"Robert, what are you waiting for?" one stray guard said aloud.

The father, Robert, stared hard. In his eyes sat cold stones in lieu of pupils. His daughter, red-faced, begged him, nevertheless.

He was a man of fine material. Knee-length breeches were worn over his stockings, darkened in color with hints of red and black to it. His tailcoat was cut high over the top of the breeches and adhered to his taut, muscular body. His collars were turned up, and a ruffled cravat was worn at his neck. He wore no hat atop his head of hair, though Garlic felt a top hat might have suited him just fine. No cloak, either, unlike the standard set used in previous centuries. Robert's overcoat was thick and furred with expensive materials.

He was not a soldier; what Garlic saw was a man off-duty but prepared for a fight all the same. Garlic would not have been surprised if leather armor rested beneath his clothes.

"What would Mom think if she saw you right now?" Cassandra's pleas had turned to blackmail. An attempt to sway his feelings with guilt. "She's suffering as it is. She doesn't need more chaos, *Robert*."

Garlic cringed as much as Robert did at the mention of his name.

He was the enemy here, but he was still her father, and the softness behind his eyes and the rush in his heart that went amiss to most was noticed perfectly by the vampire. Still, he was Captain of the Town's Guard; his insignia and emblem stitched into his shoulder was a sign of his allegiance to a local militia.

His wealth made sense, then, a product of the businesses he protected within the town and around it as a soldier of sorts.

Cassandra hoped he wouldn't lash out.

Garlic hoped the children wouldn't betray him.

She was now the last person who could prevent Garlic's capture. She met her father, eye to eye, and the first to speak was her. Not to the father who now fought an internal battle over whether or not to uphold duty or inflict pain on his flesh and blood.

Not knowing what would come next, the vampire considered his options. Beneath the wrapping of cloth that coated his body was his greatest weapon—himself. If combat was certain, then he knew it was now or never. He had to act.

Cassandra, without looking at Garlic, said calmly, "Don't act out. I promise everything will be okay. Just go along with what happens."

12

He hadn't expected to find himself in the predicament that now faced him.

He hadn't expected Cassandra's father to round up every last child for inspection… or strike his daughter, either.

Shocked faces filled his view as the stinging slap filled the air around them. Of all the choices he could've made as he stepped forward only a moment ago to wrestle his daughter away from the proposed criminal, he had opted to slap her.

Raw, red, and sharp, Cassandra's cheek felt the immense pressure behind it. The man was on edge and had chosen to do the one thing he shouldn't have. That alone made Garlic jolt forward. Cassandra held him back. She shoved her body into his and kept his back to the wall. Not a word was spoken as Robert turned to the large unit he now had at his side. The cries of Scarlett were all that could be heard.

"Take them to my estate," he muttered and looked back at Cassandra. His lips held a tremble as if he wanted to apologize. Yet, he held onto duty.

The estate wasn't along an outer field or an external plot of land off of town; instead, it lay on a fair plot within the city not far from where the group had been rounded up and forced to submit. It sat among urban riches of the wealthier district and overlooked the town, almost. It stood tall and fancy, with some parts appearing older than others. It was a mansion that had gone through renovation after renovation and now stood as a beacon of the wealthiest family in the town, with the man at the head of the household serving as the captain of the local guard. Though, its wealth wasn't derived from the father.

All her friends had quietly accepted whatever fate might come as the surrounding public watched on. Protest arose when children as small as Scarlett, held by Michael, were forced by a pack of guards past the front gates and through the luscious gardens and finally escorted through the front, large double-oak doors with gold cresting. This mansion was not a prison or even some form of local jail. This was purely a home that rested on a fancy estate.

The father saw a strange situation and dealt with it as best he could, and the group was caught unawares at the same moment that Garlic's weakness had tripped up their forward progress. The sun had caught his cheek, and now they were reaping the consequences. In his heart, he knew he had been too careless. He felt great guilt for the trouble he had caused.

Cassandra's friends said nothing to her, and Michael's frowns toward her held more shock than anything else. Garlic noticed sooner than anyone else that Cassandra's wealth had likely been exaggerated in the past. What they saw was a luxurious manor filled with kitchens, servants, great dining halls, and places of study with more wondrous paintings and windows than anyone could have ever dreamed of.

Robert, the father of the household, attempted to handle things personally. Behind locked doors, he hoped to uncover what he believed was wrong. He didn't want word to spread, nor for his name to be tarnished—though he had done that himself. Garlic saw right through the man's mindset. Now, he pondered what the consequences would be.

Garlic struggled to see it. Or her. A woman, the mother of Cassandra, with baggy eyes and a frown to her face, a droop of sorts that spelled out her exhaustion. She looked tired in a blue gown that fell to her calves.

"Did you or did you not slap my daughter, Robert?"

Garlic listened closely for the father's reply.

The echo, and sting, of another slap then echoed down the halls.

Did he strike his wife? Garlic wondered.

Quite the opposite. He noticed mere men manhandling him. It almost hurt his pride, yet he knew there were bigger things at play.

Cassandra's mother, a woman who, based on the name spoken by the people around her, was called Martha, had released a firm slap of her own that echoed throughout the halls.

The area was now crammed with bodies, and the room to move was scarce.

The murmurs of the children, teens, and the staff of this household were caught in a flurry of confusion. No one knew what was happening, or what was going on. It was chaos.

The words that came demanded answers as to why her daughter held the pained, red mark on her cheek and no answer came to his tongue. His vocal cords didn't rustle up an attempt to reply.

No one believed it. The father was brought down to a quiet grumble. He was firm and certain, though he wished he had kept his distance. From the moment they entered the estate, he had hoped to separate Garlic from the group, only for Cassandra's mother to not only get involved but provide the group a moment of respite.

Garlic was not shy as to what had happened, regardless of his view and the lack of hearing. He tried to focus, to hone the senses that some might see as the perk of being not only a vampire but essentially an apex predator. The situation may soon require more concentration and energy, both of which he, unfortunately, could not find at present. His concentration was constantly amiss, and his energy was scarce.

I need to feed soon. He shook his head. *I need to get through this city before my strength fails me… or at least, I need to rest.*

The personal guards of his manor rallied around the group. Garlic moved with them on the mother's orders. The father lost what power he had over the vampire at that moment. Garlic looked up and saw in her eyes a seething rage. Upon noticing Garlic's attention, it disappeared. Next came fascination. He couldn't get a good look at her, but the look she got of him was far too clear to be coincidental. He wasn't sure what her expression was, and he decided it was best to not think about it.

No one had expected to be taken to the father's estate and into his home, whereupon Garlic was ushered into a small chamber. He sat down. It was no prison, though the empty, spare room did well enough with a locked window covered with bars. The floor was cold, and his thoughts were tedious.

The father expected nothing as of yet. Garlic only knew that he was being treated as an outlaw of sorts. He was dragged and forced all the way but felt glad that the sun's current direction did not affect the path the guards used, nor, luckily, him.

The atmosphere in the air carried an uncertain dread. Every last one of them feared what might come next. Now, with every single child in the cell with him, he waited.

13

Time passed, the sun dipped, and the warmth of the room increased. All the bodies only created more heat, and no breeze came from the bottom of the door's slight gap.

Garlic sat cross-legged near the door. When it eventually opened, he wanted to be the only thing the guards—or soldiers—saw. Alas, it could just be the father who'd come. It didn't matter; he refused to let any of the children get questioned or hurt. They had been nothing but kind, and the last thing he wanted was for them to take the punishment instead of him. Though they were clearly all afraid of him being found out. It was still a notion no one considered.

"Children, please note that no one suspects me of being what I am." He spoke vaguely in the event guards outside the thick door were listening. It wasn't a risk he was willing to take. His head moved from left to right. He gathered everyone's attention and continued. "They likely suspect me of other crimes. It would be strange if they were somehow able to con-clude that I was something else entirely." He noted that the group seemed a bit more peaceful after his statement.

"What would they suspect you for?" Sophia asked glumly.

"A foreign outlaw. A thief. A bandit. A kidnapper? I do not know. The circumstances betray whatever context they might assume." Garlic looked at his wrapped hands. "I was ready to fight earlier," he said clearly, "and I thank you for putting your trust in me. I would not have blamed anyone for spilling the truth." Everyone looked at each other.

"Why would we do that after we have come this far?" Michael's surprise bolstered the room's confidence.

"What would you have done if we did?" Andrew's question was meek. The way he asked it, and how his face dropped, revealing a despair that he tried unsuccessfully to hide, spoke volumes.

"I do not know," Garlic lied. "Animal instinct," he said quickly, which was the truth. Much of the group didn't understand. Those who did said nothing.

"Thank you, then, all the same, for trusting in us...," Michael whispered. "And Cassandra... she knew what she was doing." Garlic saw the young man's glossy eyes and the pain he held. Garlic wished Cassandra were with them so he might thank her.

"If you had to attack them, would it have been bad?" Chris asked solemnly. Garlic looked up to the ceiling and then back at the boy. He gave a simple nod.

"It would have been self-defense." Brandon argued a point no one had brought up or realized. Leaning against the rear wall, the bulky teen sniffed and cleared his throat. "I have some questions."

"Please, do ask." Garlic peered over his shoulder at Brandon. "Anyone else may as well."

"Thank you. Sunlight hurts you, then?" It was the first real word any of them had spoken since they were thrown into the room by stoic guards, and an uncertain father, that wasn't sad in tone.

"Sunlight to me leads to an instantaneous sunburn. It's a slow, tedious burn. Just because I move out of the sun doesn't mean the damage isn't done. I have to recover from it." Garlic prodded without hesitation at the area where the new burn was. "It's still warm."

"Really?" Brandon's amazement urged him to lean forward. "This will sound strange, but can I touch it?"

Garlic sighed. He stood, though everyone else remained seated. He felt ready for anything that may come. "You are welcome to if you do not believe me."

Brandon reached out to the man who knelt, and with his right index finger extended, he leaned forward from his seated position with a slight groan to keep himself steady. He prodded the freshly burnt skin only once, and though his touch was as delicate as a mother's with a newborn, he recoiled and fell into a short laugh of sorts. It still felt hot to the touch, not that anyone else knew.

"Was it warm?" asked Garlic.

"It felt hot," Brandon declared, quenching the group's curiosity on the matter. "Does anyone else want to try?"

Garlic laughed and turned back toward the door. "I am not a toy. I shall choose whether anyone else will touch my cheek."

Silence followed.

Andrew shifted and Garlic knew *exactly* what was coming. "Can we?"

"Fine," he murmured and knelt so that everyone, one by one, from the tall Michael to the tiny Scarlett who decided it would be sweet to kiss his cheek better. He felt like a stuffed animal being played with, though the responses were kind overall.

Somehow, even against the circumstances they found themselves in within the empty, dull room, the group found a way to make light of it. Everyone turned to a comedic discussion of the sunlight, which spawned a plethora of new conversations.

Garlic stood idle by the door after that, left alone save for some occasional interactions with Scarlett. She would wander by and pry at the cloth around his legs until the question of what exactly he was wearing came up.

"He looks like a mummy," Scarlett observed.

"Of course, he does," Andrew replied. On his face sat a grin whilst Scarlett looked upset.

"Not my mummy!" she protested.

"She meant 'mummies,'" Michael corrected, and the group fell into silence.

"He looks like a… oh," Andrew realized, and the delight of the group exploded.

Of course. She was the one to tell me I looked like a mummy of ancient Egypt, and from here….

It was as he expected—the group embarked on an argument as to whether he was a mummy or not. The battle of words raged on so long he lost track of the time. Two opposing sides—those for the idea that he was a mummy and those against it—emerged. Except for one impartial individual. The one no one else paid much mind to. Cari was only one year older than Scarlett and the only one to have not voiced an opinion on the matter. In his eyes, she was the tiebreaker.

"If you all are so confident with your choices, then I say we allow the person who has not had the chance to speak as of yet be the one to decide whether or not I am a mummy." The group exchanged glances with each other, lost as to who hadn't cast their vote into the flames of the debate. "Cari should decide," Garlic said at last and left the vote to be decided by her and her alone.

She looked up, a girl as sweet as Scarlett, and spoke well through blushed cheeks and a stammer. "He… h-he… he is a mummy!"

The side who vouched that he was a mummy went into an uproar. The laughter and joy of the victorious remained for a time.

Eventually, the noise died down, and Garlic overheard more singular discussions—Brandon discussed sunlight with Chris and Luke, and his question: "Is sunlight technically able to hurt mummies too but over a longer period?" sent everyone into discussion again. This time they were more open about his status as a vampire, much to the annoyance of Michael, who knew no one suspected such a thing, outside of their room, and the last thing he wanted to happen was to be overheard by the wrong person at the wrong time. Even if everyone kept their conversations vague and strange, it was still easy to know that the topic of a "vampire" was involved.

It was then that Andrew voiced a new query. "Are we all vampires technically if sunlight hurts us too?" This spurred on the conversation, which ended in a consensus of "Yes." They were all vampires, in their opinions, much to the disappointment of Garlic.

With kind words, he urged them, "Please, do not think that way, nor dare say it either."

"But you're really nice." Sophia's words spurred the group again. Their chaotic conversations were like the ocean's waves on a violent, windy day. He couldn't keep up and soon decided to just wait and see what might happen next.

The group could laugh and joke and talk all they pleased. He knew they would likely be okay, and if they weren't, he would vouch for them. He did consider, though, that once alone, he might escape of his own accord....

I'm not far from the way I must go anyway, he thought but found no justifiable answers. In the end, there was no real way to triumph through this situation and provide everyone a sweet ending. Garlic hoped the sealed door of the chamber was thick, lest anyone overheard.

"Garlic," Abby began, drawing his attention away from the door. That door was his true enemy. He hated it with a passion. He knew he could destroy it, and then ravage his way through the manor till he escaped. That door.... He *hated* that door.

"Garlic?" a new voice called, and he spun. It wasn't new, but it wasn't Abby's either.

"Young female?" he answered and recoiled. "Uh... yes?" He had no clue as to her name. If he were honest, he didn't remember half the names of the group who protected him.

Abby, the one he expected, had shied away with Emma. Emma shied away too when he forgot her name. He wasn't sure if it had ever been mentioned either.

"For someone who lives forever, your memory is terrible," Sophia stated, blunt as a bat.

"Ah, you'd be surprised how much I have to try and remember." *For a vampire who's lived as long as the elders of the ancient world, I am amazed too, Sophia. That... was her name, wasn't it? I do not know, I'm afraid.*

"Sophia!" Abby blurted out quietly.

Sophia responded loudly, "Oh, right!"

Garlic nodded.

Sophia was the one to step forward with pride and honor. "Emma wanted to know if wooden stakes are the only way to... you know...."

"It was my question!" Abby intervened, and Garlic laughed as the group of girls nearly fell into a scrap.

Garlic shook his head. "No, anything can kill me if enough impairment is done. You would be surprised. I hate how often my attackers aim for my heart and not my head."

"What's wrong with that?" Sophia questioned, and tried her hardest to pry Emma from her arm, who in turn tried her hardest to pry Abby from hers. The triangle of shy cuteness was anything but cute. He wanted to laugh more than anything else. He didn't blame them for being nervous around the immortal vampire.

"Ah, you have posed a good question. But think of it like this: It is amusing, as a clean slice of my head will likely end me for good." Garlic watched closely for their reaction.

The three girls flinched.

"That makes no sense. Why has no one ever tried to slice your head off?" Sophia challenged.

"Because once people learn what I am…," Garlic crouched down to be at their height, "…humans tend to aim for what they *think* they know will defeat me."

"Lies," Abby whispered.

"Lies?" he repeated, interested. "What makes you say that?"

Emma and Sophia turned to the shyest girl in the room.

"Someone might have tried?" Abby pointed out.

Garlic weakened at her challenge of his point. "If anyone were to know, it would be me. Besides, no one has ever tried, at least not directly."

Abby nodded and ducked her head. "Thank you!"

He raised an eyebrow. "You're… welcome?" *Was that a bow?*

Abby's bow, though unneeded, caught the group's attention.

"Are we entering another question session?" Michael said aloud, and the group leaped at the chance like a pack of lions might charge their vulnerable prey.

The first to come forward with energy that could likely fuel a furnace was Andrew. It couldn't have been anyone else. He had come to expect the erratic boy to be the one to think of the most unusual of questions as the group fell into an intense argument as to who should be the first to ask.

Why had the quiet, shy girl been the one to ask if stakes could, when shoved into his heart, kill him? He looked at the quiet Abby who seemed… odd. She was usually so quiet, but now, after learning how he could be defeated, she seemed happy now. He thought nothing more of it mostly because he didn't want to. Especially if, in her head, she thought negatively of him. He wondered if she were secretly one of the few who, whilst they all liked him as far as he could tell, knew some of them still might see him as a predator. Regardless, Abby went on with the ongoing chatter of the group.

"I'm first!" Andrew shouted and lurched forward. "Oh, and what about bats?"

Garlic's confusion was beyond them at this point. He wished he could move his features more, as his blank, non-moving face showed no real reaction. "What about them?"

Andrew twiddled his fingers and spoke through a groan. "Can you turn into one?"

"I… uh… no, I cannot do that."

"You mean… you won't, or you can't?" Andrew pressed, as inquisitive as a cheetah in search of its next meal. He eyed the vampire with such animosity that, for an instant, Garlic felt genuinely threatened. He felt the hairs on his neck rise to the challenge of a young teen's honest question. There was nothing but innocence behind something that felt dark in the way he spoke of it.

"I… can't."

Andrew groaned even further. "Then what is the *point*?"

Garlic felt a bubble of laughter rise to his throat. "Why does humanity believe I should be able to?"

"Do you want to?" Andrew asked.

"Oh, I wish I could," Garlic said and felt a ball of hope bloom in his chest. "I would fly through the town."

"No problems then, eh?" Andrew agreed with him, slightly monotone. "It'd be fun being a bat."

Garlic shook his head. "Whilst I can't be a bat, I can speak to bats… I am more like… a 'bat man' than a vampire."

"A… bat man?" Andrew repeated.

"We should just call you the 'bat man' now," Michael called out, in a cheerier than dreary way. The boys agreed in moments and the girls were quick to do the same.

"Am I to be henceforth known as the Bat Man?" Garlic asked, curious as to whether such a unique nickname would be a genuine name for him. The group considered this. Luke was steadfast in agreement, whilst Cari and Brenna were the only two others to voice some form of an agreement. The rest all looked to Scarlett, red-faced and near tears, choked up on her words.

"Sweetheart, what's wrong?" Michael cooed to her.

"I... I... I...," she sniffed and looked at Luke angrily. "His name... is *Garlic*."

No one dared argue his name after that, and the brightness that filled her little cheeks and joyful face stamped his name in stone once again. He was happy no one protested the littlest girl's wishes. If being known as Garlic would make a little girl happy, he would make sure for certain the name stuck. Most had forgotten the "senior" part. Except for him, of course. He was happy everyone forgot the fact that he was far older than most likely even their bloodlines. He considered that reality and dismissed it.

"You talk to bats?" asked Andrew.

"Yes." It was the first time he had openly said it aloud, and at that moment, he felt strangely content to discuss it with them. *Why not?* He knew sooner or later, he'd be fighting for his life. *May as well provide them memories they'll never forget. Memories spent in an empty, oddly hot room with a waddling vampire covered in cloth....*

A thud at the door sounded, followed by a lock's *clunk*. The door, with creaks and moans, opened. The room fell silent, and the door swung open, revealing two people who stood at the threshold—a frustrated father and a dismissive daughter.

14

Garlic tensed and locked eyes with the father. A part of him still wasn't happy the man had struck his daughter. Cassandra stood by him, and the look on her face ripped him in two. Stuck between upset and angry, there was no place for any other emotion. He hoped she might smile or say something good to the group, but what she said was to him and him alone.

Her lips parted and a few bland words came forth. "Garlic, please come with me," she said as her father stood by, which implied the worse option: *us* instead of *me*. He kept himself calm and collected and gave a curt nod.

So be it, he thought.

He said nothing and followed after her, the group silently staring as the scene unfolded. The father moved aside, as did Cassandra so he might fit through the door with no trouble, and... he still got stuck. He sighed.

"May I... have a hand?" he grumbled, embarrassed almost. The father tutted and turned away as Cassandra awkwardly tugged him from the doorway.

"I'm... going to need help, please." Cassandra pulled again. "How did we even get you in the room to begin with?"

Garlic shrugged.

"Someone, help would be nice!"

"Yeah, yeah, on it… Cassandra," Michael said, being the first to answer her call, and yet he still referred to her by her full name. Michael didn't see Cassandra flinch, but Garlic did. She disliked the name. That much was clear. That name was used by those who thought she was higher or should be higher, not by those she truly cared for. She wanted to be Sandra, and the group stuck in a hot room gave her the understanding she needed to have it be so.

"Okay, ready… sir?" Michael asked.

"Uh, yes?" Garlic replied, confused as to why he had been called "sir," when it occurred to him that it was *probably* for the best that no one called him by Scarlett's given name either. It clicked in his head after that.

Cassandra has already called me "Garlic" and, well, surely her father would see that as suspicious.

"Push," Michael directed.

Garlic was nudged. Somewhat.

"This isn't working," Cassandra realized, hot and flushed as her cheeks went a rosy red. "Please, Michael, put some back into it."

"I'm putting all my back into it!"

Garlic was nudged again.

"I'm trying my hardest," Cassandra grunted. "Brandon, get over here."

"On it."

Garlic closed his eyes and wished the ordeal would be over.

"One, two…," Brandon took a deep breath. "Three!"

Garlic fell forward, knocked Cassandra to the side, and rolled to the ground. He tumbled on until he finally found his footing.

"You all can stay here," Cassandra's father commanded. Garlic caught the view of Michael and Brandon backing away from the door without a word. It was also the first time in a long time that Michael gave a small, lopsided grin to Cassandra… and the flash of hope on her face was something to be treasured.

Do I live now for drama? Garlic huffed as he finally got off his knees and back on his feet. *I've been alive too long… I need a holiday. Where haven't I been? Perhaps I should just speak to them honestly about their want for the other?*

"Garlic," Cassandra began as the door shut and locked with a *kerchunk*, "let's get moving?" She spoke more as if it were a question than a call to action. He felt tempted to say no. Yet her father stood nearby, peacefully at least. Garlic looked in his eyes. Internally, the man seemed livid but conflicted.

I assume the anger you feel, Captain, is for yourself.

He stepped forward, and the father backward. Garlic shot a glance at Cassandra and her swollen left cheek. It was the first time he had noticed it since they had arrived. The mark of the man's calloused hand where it had hurt her was clear. It still looked raw and sharp to the touch, but she seemed to think nothing of it.

She directed him to move, and his innocent floundering was ignored by the father, who walked ahead of them both. Not a single guard nor patrol was near them.

So, no one heard our talks inside.... Garlic followed after the man with Cassandra by his side. Silence passed between the awkward trio. Following the father's footsteps down empty halls, he thought, *We must be in some kind of backroom. Or storage area. It's rather barren.*

A sudden, outspoken voice broke the silence. "My daughter tells me that you are a performer from another land. She tells me that you are here to put on a show for the people and that my daughter was taking you to my wife to inquire about such a thing." The father with cold eyes peered over his shoulder at Garlic.

I hope you, if you are as fair a man as the people of this town believe, will reconcile with your daughter.

Garlic said nothing in return. A quick thought told him that if that was the backstory Cassandra had created, it was best that he abide by it. He knew what was happening was a test. To be told the story Cassandra created outright was suspicious. Garlic eyed the man with caution. By telling the story, he knew he was giving Garlic a chance to improvise if there was something at play.

Lies lurked. That much was obvious. Her father assumed an investigative perspective. His actions made him distant.

Whatever plans you once had, Robert, were ruined the moment we got into your household. I am sorry that you'll be the one to suffer the consequences of your actions.

He considered how Cassandra's mother saw an end to her husband's rash actions, and Garlic began to surmise that the father had lost. He understood the man's actions had led to this result, but what he did and continued to do was sow resentment.

Say her name, at least.

The father looked ahead. "I know what you are thinking." His voice, dark and cold, went low. "I did what any father and any protector of this town would, so please, do not be discouraged from a staged performance in the central square should my wife enjoy your company."

Garlic perked up and cast a glance at Cassandra. She was just as thrilled to realize that the one thing they wanted most had happened: Her father had taken the bait.

He's truly a fool, then? Garlic looked from him to his daughter. *Could it truly be this easy?*

"You see, the town is on high alert. I can only be honest and admit to you that I have heavily been on edge today. It is this exact reasoning that led me to be reckless with you. I should have been more logical. See, we've had rumors…," the father peered at Garlic. "Rumors of an assassin."

"Oh?" Garlic muttered as a reply. He didn't care for the rumor; all he wanted to know was who had started it and why. He did have a target; so, the rumor of an assassin wasn't exactly… *incorrect.*

"Indeed. The rumor came from a city near here. They put out a reward for anyone who might appear out of place. As a result, I've been patrolling in places I ordinarily wouldn't be."

"Ah, is this why I saw you so far from home earlier today?" Garlic asked. Cassandra stood idly by and kept her pace a little bit behind them.

Robert grunted an affirmative. "Yes. The *lesser* side of the town isn't normally given such strict supervision. Not many guards want to patrol this grimmer, poorer side of life." The father held his head high. "It seems to me that if there were an assassin, I'd expect him to come through the rear of the town from the old roads where the forest and swamps meet. I had a plan to leave us open on our rear side to make the assassin venture into town and catch him unawares where we're strictest." The father went lax, his shoulders loosened; his tone lost its proud edge. "And, as a result, all I've done is cause turmoil and upset outsiders.... My apologies."

Garlic blinked as puzzle pieces crashed into place. "Ah...of course."

Everything made all too much sense. His gaze met Cassandra's, who looked absolutely horrified now that she had learned the truth and heard her father's blunt words. More puzzle pieces clicked, and Garlic understood now just how much her father was dismissive of those "beneath him." He imagined he would have never taken kindly to Michael and his group if she had come forward at the beginning with the truth. Though little made sense still, and he hoped to learn more.

They took a turn, and a great, deep, echoing sense of dread rippled through Garlic's soul. It threatened with snarls and groans to tear him in two. To end him. To break him. A baleful warning to not come closer. To not dare risk even looking in its direction.

The awful sense of foreboding screamed at him as he walked by it, and his heart wrenched. It twisted and croaked. His body went stiff. Beads of sweat dropped off him. Every last inch of his gut felt sick as a bubbling liquid formed in his throat. His eyes went bloodshot. His skin paled against the burns and tan.

15

The father noticed none of Garlic's suffering. But Cassandra did.

Garlic walked by a built-in church the prestigious family manor held under its roof, and then, as they passed it by, his torment disappeared as if nothing had happened.

He breathed heavily. Hand clutched at his heart, he wondered what horrible twist of luck might have taken place for him to end up in a situation as sickening as this. To walk past the church of God. Of the Almighty. It struck such a fear in him that he had no control. It made him bury his feral instinct down. It made him want to curl up and run as far as his body would allow.

"Cassandra, you may take him the rest of the way." Robert stepped to the side. "I have to go and... speak to your *friends*." The father watched as the two walked by him, not sparing another look at the man.

They walked and walked until Cassandra sighed. They turned a corner. "He means that he doesn't want to face the wrath of my mother, and he has to go and apologize to my friends so that their parents don't come parading over in protest of his reckless actions." Cassandra, despite the shockingly bad luck she'd had today, kept her head high. He respected her for that... while still recovering from his run-in with God.

The bruise was in clear view, and she chose to leave her white, muddied dress unchanged. She had made her choice of living a double life too. Everyone had a choice, he knew. Then, the realization hit him.

I'm seeing her mother? He wondered to what extent the lie had been taken. Regardless, he knew he was in for a game of "Who's the best actor?" wherein he would be the actor, and the others involved would be clueless. For someone who'd lived God-knows-how-long, you'd think such a situation wouldn't have filled him with anxiety—but it did. He wasn't good with words when confronted. Most confrontations ended the same way. Still, for now, he had one question on his mind.

"May I ask why you continued to call me by the name the little one gave me?"

Cassandra looked at him. "The little one? Scarlett?"

"Yes," he answered.

Cassandra looked ahead of them. "Oh, well, he asked for your stage name. I said you were playing the role of 'Garlic,' which is meant to be the, uh, homeless person." She bowed her head at him apologetically. "I'm sorry. I panicked when he asked."

Garlic stared at her. "Well, did he accept that reason?"

She held her head high. "Y-yes, he did…." Bit by bit, her head began to lower again. "I don't know what to do… I've tried my best."

He focused again on the poor girl's truth. She was torn between worlds, it seemed, but in her heart, she was trying to mend things. "All will be well in the end," he promised her. "You've done well to maintain things and continue to do so."

"I just wanted to help…."

He wasn't sure who or what exactly her meek words were directed at. "Cassandra?"

"Just Sandra, please."

"*Sandra*, did you know that I can't go through life without avoiding things such as silver?"

She blinked twice and then looked ahead and behind before she replied quietly, "Um… yes, I think? Most tales list silver as a weakness of… people such as yourself."

He gave her a tough gaze and kept his voice low. "Yes. Silver hurts. A testament to my curse. See, anything can hurt me and kill; only silver is different, not because of what it is, or what it does, but because of how I perceive it in my mind. To me, it is beautiful and makes for fantastic apparel and other uses too that I will never be able to touch nor get near. Ironic, I suppose?"

Cassandra kept her head high. "What point are you trying to make, sir?"

"My point…," *I feel so old….* "My point is that…." *What is my point?*

Cassandra tutted, a sound similar to the noise her father had made when Garlic got stuck in the doorway. "I hope this building doesn't scare you. We've got silver in everything, nearly." A grin flashed his way, teasing him. "Or are you feeling unwell?"

He shook his head. "It isn't always the silver directly. It also happens when the silver reflects light. The effect is similar to that of sunlight when it touches my skin."

She nearly stopped at that. "And yet, you wish to hold and use it?"

"Yes."

"The silver?" she clarified.

"Yes."

"You would want to hold and use that which hurts you?"

"Of course," he confirmed. They journeyed down a long corridor filled with telltale signs of luxurious living. "Even now, look at this…." The two passed a large mirror set firmly onto the wall, and they gazed at the glass in unison. She was confused, whilst he waited. It took a while for the realization to hit. She gasped, for she could not see him. His reflection wasn't visible to either of their eyes.

"I can't see you."

"Indeed, and yet, if the mirror isn't made with silver, I can see myself. Often enough, it is nice to see how I look… when it's not through the reflection of a puddle." He looked longingly into the mirror and turned away.

"Of blood?" she asked with a fair voice.

He sighed. "Of blood," he confirmed. "Should we move on?" he urged her so they wouldn't be caught staring at his non-existent reflection. "And even then, I'd never let good blood go to waste… unless they were anemic."

Cassandra copied his pace, then took a slight lead so that she could properly lead him to their destination. "Sorry, what was that?"

"Anemic."

Cassandra looked at him with a curious gaze. "May I ask what that is?"

He nodded and understood. The world hadn't made the progress needed to be aware of such things. For how old he was, he often forgot how many personal "advancements" he chose to undertake himself in the world of medicine and science. Though, history had often proven that whenever he tried to help humanity using thousands of years-worth of experience, he was often refused, outed, or accused of some form of heresy.

"Think of it as someone who has a lacking in blood. A better term would be 'unhealthy blood,'" Garlic explained.

"I see," Cassandra responded and mused over the thought of "unhealthy blood" until she murmured, "Yes, but why?"

He pulled back his lips into a half-hearted smile, then grimaced. "Blood of that variety is a last-ditch effort, so to speak. I had promised myself that were I even on the brink of starvation, I'd never stoop so low as to drink anemic blood."

"You would truly rather starve?" She couldn't believe it and the rolling of her eyes said as much.

"No, no, truly. You become cursed as I was, and be as I am. When you can only truly survive off the blood of a human, I would dare you to drink that type of blood yourself. You'll understand, then, just how oddly grim it is…."

"If you were going to die, would you drink it?"

"I refuse to drink it." The two, through playful comments, challenged one another down the halls of her home.

"I do not believe if you were dying that you'd not drink it."

He drew in a deep breath, expelling it soon after with a glare in her direction. "I've even tried to steer certain prey onto a good diet so that they might help themselves."

"Truly?" she said, caught in the realm of disbelief. "You'd go through the effort to put prey on a good diet and healthy lifestyle before you'd risk it?"

"Always."

A door they passed flung open, and from within burst forth a maid who held a tray of garlic.

With a speed neither of the ladies could follow, Garlic chucked himself down the hall, gasping as he did so in a frantic, puzzling mess.

"My lady," the maid muttered. "What…? Who…?"

"Uh, he's a friend," Cassandra said, and carried on her way, grabbing Garlic as they went. "For someone named Garlic," she muttered into his covered ear, "you sure don't like it."

"I'm allergic," he countered and looked back at the confused maid, who shook away her thoughts and carried on.

"Allergic?" She giggled softly. "Are you sure it isn't just your… curse?"

"Probably, but I'd rather not risk it either way. Ever. Young lady."

They turned one last corner, and the hallway took them toward a single entrance where two large oak doors led into a grand room with a grand table and grand velvet carpet. "My mum said she'll meet you here," Cassandra said and gestured for him to go inside. "I'll be waiting outside for you."

"Am I safe, Sandra?" he asked her. "I have come to trust your group… and I have placed my faith in you."

Cassandra's face lit up like a firework. "You may trust me…. Thank you."

He bowed as far down as he could. "Then… I'll enter."

"Best of luck…."

He went inside without another word, accepting his fate to act his part as a foreigner who had come to conduct business.

"Best of luck," she whispered a second time for some reason unknown. He walked inside. The doors closed behind him. The near pitch-black room was a beautiful space to him. He welcomed the looming darkness. Relaxed, he wandered the room, perfectly adapted to the darkness until he chose the furthest end of the long table and took a seat on the cushioned, sturdy chair.

He waited and waited. Time passed. He knew not how much, though. The darkness beckoned to him further, till he heard the two doors open and then close, followed by footsteps that rattled through the room. He saw the outline of the person, though he wagered the other person couldn't see him. He focused, utilizing the abilities he boasted and detested, and saw her in greater detail. Though he was still mystified as to the true look of the person in question.

He licked his chapped lips. He fiddled with a nearby fork made of something not quite silver. Strategically placed as he seemed to be, he noticed the room's darkness, the lack of mirrors, silver, and people. It felt set up to near perfection for someone who, perhaps, might be a vampire.

"I know you're in here." A woman with a fair voice, sore and slightly afraid, said, "I know you are here."

The scorching light of a lit candle forced him to grip the armrests of his chair; his strength crushed the wood into dust and splinters. The woman, in the flicker of light that fought the dim of the dark, saw him and rested her baggy eyes peacefully on his form. It was as if to see him brought her peace. For him to see her brought nothing but alarm. "I never thought I'd see the day…."

The woman wore a silky blue gown. Her hair was tied up and across her face rested a soft, yet stubborn look much like her daughter's. The wrinkles were clear, and she appeared tired—lacking sleep. He had been unable to gather a good look the last time he saw her. So, to see her now….

"You appear exhausted. Shall we conduct this meeting another day?"

"Don't play such games, vampire. My daughter has said many things to secure your safety. Don't worry. You'll have it." The lady took the lit candle and brought it with her toward the table and sat across it, easing into the chair that sat opposite his. Eyes narrowed with fierce anxiety, he stared deeply at the holy cross that sat around her neck.

16

"You hate it, do you not?"

Her bluntness caught him off-guard. "We are still so far. How do you know I stare?"

"Because the glare reflected by the cross around my neck from the candle is enough."

He stared at the cross that made his eyes sore. "Its mere presence is enough, milady."

The lady scoffed. "And why's that?"

He ignored her mention of "vampire" from earlier. He hoped to fight his battle verbally, if not for his sake, then for the group of mismatched people who had gotten him this far.

"I do not know why."

She spoke fast. "Are you religious?"

He ruffled his cloth and bit the inside of his cheek. "I am. I wish I could visit the church and pray and be baptized…. It is a strong faith, a way to find hope and redemption for all that I do…." *She kept the room dark. I knew from the moment I entered that the lady I was to meet had planned for this. She is aware of my truth and has acted accordingly.* "I detest it, though. The curse I am reflects from the holy cross, and it binds me, breaks me, and beats me."

The lady giggled something soft. Like Cassandra. There was no ill intent. He took this as a sign to be cautious.

"Do you hope one day for a fair trial?" The lady fiddled with the silver cross around her neck and relaxed into her seat as if they had been friends for a long time.

"I hope that when my time comes to die that God will accept me and cure me of my ailments, and then, only then, will I atone for my sins as a true mortal." Nervous, he raised a bandaged-covered arm and hand and pointed directly at her cross. "Please, may you hide it from my view?"

"Of course." Slowly, she tucked it away into the hem of her dress until it rested against the right side of her chest.

"Enough games, milady," he demanded at last. "Who are you?"

She lowered her head and spoke with a sweet touch to her tongue. "When I was a little girl, I met someone who told me that vampires aren't nasty, gory, and loathly. The man I met proved to me that what humanity might consider being evil was polite, well-mannered, and preferred his prey unconscious and unable to feel pain as the blood was drained from their body. Even if the person is already dead without your intervening, the blood remains good for a few minutes after death. I remember you joking once that you were going to suck it all out anyway. Yet… you taught me that you prefer no mess. A meal is a meal to you, the same way a meal to a human can often be a treat. You told me that blood type makes a difference. Can you think of how that might make a little girl question everything she has ever known? Wonder over the knowledge you might have. You told me not just that, but general health affects the quality, and someone lacking iron in their blood can be bland and tasteless—and lucky, as you have standards. You told me that you try not to be picky when hunger is hunger and survival becomes survival. You told me, truly, that you are no different from the animals and the same people who hunt them."

She stopped.

He stared.

She gulped.

He feared.

"Is this true?" she pressed.

His memory was left in ruins. She had made him a wreck in his search for answers. "Perhaps."

She released a happy groan. "For years I've carried knowledge I was unsure of...."

He didn't feel threatened... but he didn't feel comfortable either. *To think my worries when I sat down was how I was going to get back up again with all these cloth pieces on me.* "You know me?"

"Yes. We met once when I was a little girl. I found you, and you were brutally honest. You had escaped a fight and were dying. You told me that you can only survive on humans. We argued, and I tried to give you other foods, but you told me then that someone will have to die sooner or later because you have to feed. The same way a hungry lion might mark a zebra as it walks its way, the hunt begins. That primal instinct takes over." She went weak for a moment. "And… you felt torn between your sophisticated self and your animal self because of instinct." Martha smiled. "You still don't dress well… mostly rags. Hot and sweaty, I presume?"

His mouth was near agape. "Indeed…," his mind rummaged for answers and thought of one but couldn't piece everything together. *Who…? Who…? How?*

"You look homeless."

Garlic placed his hands on the edge of the table. He wasn't sure why, but the adrenaline spike was fair. "Homeless assumes I have no home nor work. One of those is true."

"Ah. You are employed?"

He considered the answer. *She somehow already knows me from the past.* "Yes."

Martha rubbed at her tired eyes. "And tell me, what is it you are here for, then?"

"To get to the other side of town. My contract takes place on the other side, at the next city over. I do not remember the name."

"A contract?" She hoped for an answer while he provided none. "You have a target, correct?"

He shifted in his seat. "Potentially."

She eyed him. "You're an assassin?"

He said nothing.

"Do you feel guilty about the things you have done?"

He clenched at the table. "I… like to believe I am in a morally bound gray zone. I go with the flow of life, as uncaring as can be." His honesty made her spring upward.

"You said exactly that once. You told me that at heart, you are not some heartless monster, but more so that after an eternity of the same way of life, acceptance is just easier."

I say that to people who treat me kindly before I leave them to their finite lifespan.

Garlic, pushed to the edge of his seat, finally murmured aloud, "I can't place my finger on how you know me."

The lady of the manor raised her hands. "You met me once when I was a little girl in the same city you are going to." She brought her elbows upon the table and cradled her chin in her interlaced hands. "I remember mothers screaming out that God will burn you and that you should feel guilt for the things you had done until I found a strange, half-naked man lying in a pile of hay in the barn."

He smiled at last. The memory shot through his mind like a lightning bolt, and the puzzle pieces fell into place. "I remember you...."

She nodded and smiled a warmness from across the table. Her tired gaze betrayed her. "You taught me that you are a survivalist doing what needs to be done." Martha near scoffed. "However, you fought so hard back then not to feel the cold, blunt feel of a rounded pellet in your flesh."

"I've lived for quite a few thousand years. I've seen all corners of humanity, and I was content with fire and steel being my worst nightmares. I refuse to be touched by modern weaponry. Gunpowder and rifles and whatever else.... Imagine that you've watched the ancient Egyptians build their pyramids and you think that is the greatest wonder you'll ever see. A few thousand years later, and I see such weapons. Mankind has advanced quicker in the past one hundred years than in all the previous centuries combined. I fear those things... I fear what will happen to my body should I be struck by a stray bullet. Whether it be cannon fire or a volley from flintlock rifles, I *refuse* to be shot." Garlic, stirred, shaken, and nervous, relaxed slightly.

Martha stared at him with wide eyes. "I've never seen someone be so riled up from a fear of... pistols and rifles."

"It'll only get worse, I wager." Garlic looked deep into her eyes. "I fear what humanity will create in the next one hundred years."

"Long after I'm gone?"

"Indeed."

Martha and Garlic met each other's gaze once more. She saw an immortal entity left in a paranoid fear of the way the world had changed and would continue to do so.

"And if people understood and helped me—if they offered up their recently dead, though no one ever will, I could live peacefully."

He knew exactly how that exchange went back then when they had first met. He remembered how he had offered her that exact same argument when she was just a little girl. But, back then, with how young she was and how kind she was, much like her daughter, he had seen a flare in her just like Cassandra had, and he understood it all at last.

"I told you it was fair, though, as I tried to help you up as you bled from horrific wounds." She shook her head at him. "You stand by the same ideal?"

He hummed. "You'll have to be specific. What was fair?"

She cocked her head to the left. "That it is only fair no one does offer up their dead, as a dried-up corpse is never a nice way to remember someone they loved when they were among the living."

He remembered her perfectly now, the memory in clear view in his mind. He remembered surviving the fight of a lifetime and having a city hellbent on seeing his end when a young girl in a barn found a man in a bloodied haystack. He remembered how cool he felt, the chill on his body as the warmth left him, not that he had much to begin with.

He looked at the table in defeat. He wished he could've given her a memory that was far more cheerful than the one she had dealt with for years and years.

"I make my living as an assassin. I kill them, drink them, and hide the body. No one ever knows. My life and employment sustain me."

She bobbed her head in full agreement. Leaning back, she rested against the rear of the chair. "Of course, I wouldn't question that… but know there are people like my daughter and I who think differently."

"And your husband?" Garlic's inquisitive tone made her shift and ruffle her gown. *Uncomfortable?* he thought and knew why. "I know already that word was sent out. A rumor of an assassin among your local elite. Your husband mentioned that already."

Her eyes, once elsewhere, shot back at him. "Did he, now?" She shifted again. "You already know then that the town is on high alert."

"Specifically on the *side* of importance too," he said and noted what he already knew to be true. "Not because of a report of a vampire or because your wealth is present here, is it?"

She shook her head, a sadness in her tone. "Rumor spread from the city I expect you are heading to. It's far, still, and the road you need will take you right to it, I presume?"

He bowed his head partly. "It is my employment. I do what I must to avoid wild hunts in the night."

"Well, they were right, then. An 'assassin' is passing through my town. Or, perhaps, 'outlaw.'" She giggled out a shrill, pained noise. "Ah," she gasped and coughed to clear her throat, "though the irony is that it would be *you*...."

"Indeed," he agreed. He narrowed his gaze. "Do you have information as to how this information slipped out?"

"Ask your employers," she mentioned slyly, almost a picture-perfect mimic of the way Cassandra might have voiced the same comment. "I'm assuming there is a traitor in your line of work."

"Perhaps. That would be so." Garlic wanted to groan as the puzzle pieces fell together. *If no rumor spread, I might've had an easier time slipping through....* He thought nothing more of it. As far as he was concerned, he had his job and nothing more.

"Does the man you hunt deserve it?"

"Somewhat."

She nodded. "I can take a gander as to who, but I'd rather not."

"Hmm. Probably for the best."

17

The conversation began to go stale as the reality of his being began to surface. He was, as she knew, a vampire. And, as all living creatures must, he had to feed. She understood the particular way in which he did, though. She presumed the very tight-knit organizations he belonged to would rather keep the immortal being in check to keep him from causing issues.

Not only was his knowledge a formidable asset but his expertise was no doubt considered beneficial as well to his employers. She smiled, impressed, for reasons she didn't know. She respected Garlic, who remained idle, watching her every move. She was fascinated by him and enjoyed the careful stares she received. She smiled wider.

"As you are a superior hunter, I feel they made a good choice to go into business with you."

"Indeed. All my targets have a tag attached when they become my responsibility. I may drink them."

"Until they are dry?" she asked.

"Until they are dry," he confirmed.

She hummed. "Providing food as reward or some form of payment," she mused, then felt a tinge of pink on her cheek at the hardy chuckle that passed her lips. "You should dispose of the bodies more often," she chided. "All too common is it for distant rumors from faraway lands to bring words and whispers of a 'vampire' targeting high-profile individuals. A body drained of blood is highly suspicious, wouldn't you say?"

Garlic groaned aloud.

"Problem?" she wondered.

"My employer has often reprimanded me for not cleaning up properly after myself. I don't often have that much time after the bells ring of an intruder." He relaxed into his seat. "Still, I am more than just a vampire hunting my prey."

The mother tutted, and a quietness brewed for a moment. In that same moment, she knew she enjoyed his company whilst he began to suspect her. The one thing he was unsure of was her intentions with him. He didn't enjoy discussions that regarded his employment in any way. The notion of her being an insider didn't worry him. He remembered her clearer, now, as the scared yet dopey and curious little girl from many, many years ago.

He felt compelled to go on. "Ah, but… the issue is more so that when a group of humans decides as a collective that the right thing for the group or the future of the children is something morally wrong—people can suddenly side with them and understand and provide sympathy. But for me? I'm an animal driven by instinct. I'm no different from the fox that tries to pick out a chicken to eat. I'm just living this life… and at this point, I'll keep doing it, no matter what people think." Garlic found it strange. His memory of her was short to him, though he now saw the impact it had on the lady. She was only a young girl back then and had apparently been blemished ever since. Yet he also saw goodness in her. Something was different.

"Of course, I hope you are teaching all of those children in a far kinder manner. I was left both scarred and open-minded for the rest of my life after I met you. You never even gave me your name. I always questioned if you were real and thought myself insane."

That was the difference. He didn't know her name either. He didn't remember her till now. She was one of many he had encountered. Yet he understood her pain. She looked tired. Awful and tired. He wondered what nightmares plagued her each night and if it were he who was in them as he existed in a memory so faint she questioned its existence.

"You look no different from the day we met…," she breathed a gentle sigh. "Yet, I'm a grown woman."

"I'm sorry," he said, voice near a whisper. "This is what I have to do and what I'll continue to do. Even if the times changed, I believe it would make no difference. It comes down to the same issue every single time—I need to drink and survive off humans. Everyone always brings up the suggestion: 'Drink animals,' but I detest them. I gain no nutritional value from animals."

She laughed at his sudden outburst, from the apology to the scattered, defensive musings on how he protected his moral and philosophical viewpoint. "It's no different from a human trying to live off the ice. That's what you told me back then."

"It is still true now," he replied. He wondered how best to put her mind to rest. He didn't want her to envelop herself in the mystery of him since it had already caused her issues in life. "Yes, it may sustain you for a little bit... but it's cold, makes your teeth ache, gives your brain a freeze. It is unpleasant and has to be done in such vast, messy amounts.... Well, who wants to live in such a manner? No one, I assume. Why should I be subjected to that if no one else is willing to change?" His arguments revealed insecurities, and it was a reminder as to why he preferred not to socialize with those kind enough to help them understand him. Their questions broke him down. He was still human in a way and parts of him were chipped away with each word that passed between them.

"You expect people to change?"

The silence was his best offense as she broke him down further.

"Vampire, all I want you to know is how glad I am that we met again.... I do not expect happy reunions. My life is bleak. Yet I am happy. I feel like I can sleep easier." Martha watched him with awe. "When you depart and say goodbye, please leave them with something far happier than you did me. I feel as if, after so many years, I wish you'd given me some advice or a warning. It wasn't the idea of what you almost did back then, it was everything afterward. I was ridiculed beyond compare. It motivated me, yes, and still... I... sorry."

Flustered, she lost her tongue, and her words became a shambled mess. He understood vaguely what point she hoped to make and felt only all the more guilty for it. If they hadn't met under such terrible circumstances, he felt it might've been better. Yet even then, as he watched the woman slip delicate droplets from her eyes, her tears poured. He felt a feeling he'd felt a hundred times before and it was one that he was glad never grew old, or he feared it would mean he was numb inside.

She was not the first person who had suffered due to discovering his existence and then living with it afterward. He felt guilt. A strong, *deep* guilt. It was only another testament to his solitary ideology. By adhering to a solitary lifestyle, he couldn't hurt anyone. He wouldn't have to sit in a room with someone who had to protect his secret or save the lives of those he'd have to kill to escape, most likely. Yet, he felt that the pain of guilt forever resided in him.

"Moments like this make me fear for my humanity.... You'd think an eternity of suffering would make me heartless, and yet...." He averted his gaze, looking at everything in the room but her. "I feel as if moments like these keep this heart of mine in check.

Though, I do feel that it is partly selfish of me in a way."

Martha choked on her words in reply, "W-what? In a... way?"

"I am cursed. You might remember that from when we first met. I feel as if, regardless of the curse, that the person who did this to me might've imagined I'd lose myself and become a feral beast of sorts. To give in to that temptation would be... most favorable. It might result in my demise. Only, I want to live. I enjoy my life somehow. I just wish there was a way, sometimes, that I could meet those who cursed me and tell them that I have not lost my way. At least, not any less than I already have at points." He sighed and leaned backward. "I'm sorry for the monologue...," he chuckled. It was weak but fair. "Thank you for listening to an immortal being's sadness and dilemma."

She giggled; the sound was as soft and weak as his own laugh. They laughed together like that for a moment, and when it passed, a sense of resolution rested in them both. Even if, for him, this moment was yet one more in an ongoing series of them, this lady may finally get a good night's sleep because of what had just transpired.

"I...," he looked at the exhaustion in her eyes. He had many, many questions. He wondered how and why she was where she was. But they knew better. This was not a happy reunion, as she had said. This was nothing more than validation on her part and realization on his. "I will do my best to depart from the children kindly, on the condition that you speak with them all and teach them, so that they may avoid the mistakes you made as well as my own."

"Thank you… I will, with every inch of my soul."

She gave such a warm, sweet smile. For a moment, he saw someone with a beauty shrouded by suffering. "I will put you and the group on the right path. Set them straight, as, like me, they will never forget you."

Slowly, he stood from his seat the same way that she had. "Of course… milady."

She smirked. "You don't remember my name?"

He stared. *I heard it earlier, I swear. Alas…I….*

He felt terrible. "No, I do not."

"You need only ask…," she grasped the base of the candle and held it up in front of her. "I feel you don't need to know. Live with wonder. You'll have plenty of time to do so."

He smirked at her, amused and proud. "So be it. Am I free to leave?"

"Of course. I need to speak with my husband."

With slow, heavy steps, he waddled across the length of the room, attempted a bow, and then gave the lady one last honest smile. "Thank you," he told her. "You've saved me twice in one lifetime. Consider yourself a rarity." His final words to her lit her once paled, tired face with pure happiness. She truly was rare to have met the same eternal vampire twice, and he definitely considered her so.

He moved for the door, placed his hand upon the large brass knob, and slowly twisted it. With a gasp of air, the left door opened whilst the right remained shut.

"Thank you," he said and spoke with honest gratitude. "Thank you…."

The mother urged him onward and said nothing more to him. "Cassandra, take the northern route under the tunnels. There will be a boat there for him."

Cassandra, who had been sitting on the floor in front of the door, leaped upward. "Y-yes, Mother."

"Don't wait."

Cassandra nodded, and without another word, beckoned for Garlic to follow.

Garlic walked with her, and as the sun began to set, he wished for the chance to slip away his cloth and become as agile as a panther in the night.

She wants me to help them… to teach them. Garlic looked over his shoulder and slowed. Cassandra turned the next corner on the way back to the group. She hadn't seen him stop. Whilst she hurried onward, he gazed backward with concerned eyes. *Stay safe and well.* He gave a bow and turned away before the woman could do anything. He saw how she watched him leave, and the tears that glistened on her pale cheeks.

18

I don't know what more I can teach these kids. Michael and Sandra, however.... He looked at Cassandra, who set to closing the doors to the kitchens and the secluded church so that he may run by with ease. *The least I can do is try and fix what was broken today by me being here. I've spoken with Michael already.* He slowed his pace so she could match his. *I haven't spoken to her.*

He wondered if it was his place to fix the argument between Michael and Cassandra. He felt responsible, and the mother's wishes only furthered that thought in his mind.

"Sandra… you have a close-knit group around you," he said as they turned the next corner and put themselves on a direct route toward the back rooms.

"You do not have to spare me advice," she replied through winded breaths. Their jog wasn't one she was used to, and the day for her had already been long and tiring. He, however, felt nothing, and her fatigue reminded him of the few perks that came with being what he was.

"I want to keep you and your group together— please do realize how truly lucky you are to have them."

"Why n-now?" she stammered. "I do not need help."

He slowed, and she did too. "It is not paltry advice I give, Sandra. My advice to you is to see it for what it is. I have made many a friend in my lifetime, so many that a time comes where I must sit back and wonder the harm it does to an eternal mind, to see time take the people I love again and again whilst I remain untouched."

Cassandra stopped and leaned against the wall for support. "Are you… trying to give me love advice?"

"No, it is unneeded." He looked forward and then behind them. "But if love is on your mind, then know you should take it when ready."

She laughed amicably at his advice. "You are strange, Garlic. All my life, I had thought vampires might be creatures to be admired. Handsome, seductive…," she spared a glance at him. "Are you saying that you have never fallen in love?"

Garlic loathed ever receiving the question he dreaded. He loved to love. Time didn't care, however. "Love for me is too scarring when time holds no value. When time holds value, it makes merit on every choice I, and we, make. For me, love is a choice that holds too little long-term value, for an eternal heartache overtakes me once it is done." His words tore a hole in her heart and bore deep into her soul.

"Are there those you… miss?"

He nodded and looked away. "Now and forever."

Cassandra nearly whimpered and pushed off the wall to bounce into him.

He blinked. *She's hugging me?* He made no response nor action, and she didn't linger either. The hug was short and somehow bittersweet.

"Thank you," he spoke quietly.

She hummed a soft song and turned away. "I'm sorry," she said and nothing more as she continued down the hall.

He walked behind her casually but felt weak of heart. His mind raced for the memories of those he had never forgotten. "Do not wait, I beg you, because one day, it might be too late for you."

"It is such basic, common advice, Garlic.... Why does it feel so much more important when it comes from you?" She didn't look at him, and though her head was held high, it seemed tilted a bit too far. Tears were held back, and her pace was now quicker than his so he couldn't see them. He felt great guilt for her sadness but knew that somewhere in her mind now echoed a voice that would reflect on this lesson learned.

Upon arriving at the back room, they found the door closed but unlocked. They opened it and found the group immersed in a quiet discussion inside. When they opened the door to reveal all was well, they asked themselves if Robert had unlocked the door at a point unknown and left without a word.

None questioned it but thought it better to stay and wait.

Cassandra looked between them all and spent a second too long on Michael. "We've all had a chaotic day, but now Garlic will tell us what I believe is good news."

Garlic stepped forward. "Cassandra's mother offered me the choice of staying and causing unrest or leaving quietly in the night. I chose to take my leave as needed. She has told me to go north to an underground passage that Cassandra will lead me to." Garlic looked back at Cassandra. "I meant Sandra."

She gave a curtsy in gratitude of him using her preferred nickname.

The group sprang up, primed for action. It was all a downhill run from there as the children and teenagers tore down the halls with a fervor of cheers and laughter.

The sun had set by then and the vampire's internal instinct had awakened. He felt fresh, new, and ready as if it were a new day. They moved toward the northern wall, then the towers, and finally the gate.

Cassandra stopped them just before the border guard. She shushed them, and the group fell into a hushed stance. They worked their way backward, maneuvering around patrols and night watchmen alike. The security was as heavy as anticipated, though finding ways to slip through was easier than expected.

To battle the darkness of the night, great flaming bonfires were held within iron baskets; the shimmers of the light not only cast great shadows for when guards were close by on their patrol but also kept the majority of the security within the vicinity of the northern wall, where guards had the best visibility. The underground passage itself wasn't far and sticking to the shadowed paths and darkened alleys was easier said than done.

Garlic took point at one turn, where Cassandra knew the route, it was he who could use his abilities best at night to guide them. Where she gave the directions, he planned the route and made sure that everyone was safe and sound on their little escapade.

"Here, here," Cassandra said and rushed the group one by one into the underground tunnels, the steps long and wide with a bit more of a drop than expected. Brandon went first, with the youngest in the middle whilst at the rear stood three quiet souls: Michael, Cassandra, and Garlic.

"Michael, after you," Cassandra said, tone as mushy as the look he gave her.

"Garlic should go first," he murmured. Both looked at the vampire.

At last, he felt the time was right. "I shall go first, but… may I know the reasoning behind why you and the others either didn't question the posh, rich girl with them or anything else beyond that until now?"

"And why would the immortal being care?" Michael retorted playfully.

Did I touch a nerve? he thought. "I'm being nosy," he admitted. "I've lived a long time. Interpersonal drama is still interesting, no matter how many times I become immersed in it—as long as there's a good resolution."

Michael peered toward Cassandra and then gazed around the local area, on the lookout for trouble. "All right. Let's make it quick," he muttered and turned to Cassandra, a guilty look on his face. "See, Cassandra isn't able to be with us as often as you'd believe. We rarely see her around, and for her to join us is actually more so a rarity. We began the game of hide-and-seek today at my request." Michael looked at the curious Garlic and the confused Cassandra. "You said you had to go, so… I brought up hide-and-seek so everyone would get excited, and you'd want to stay."

Cassandra cocked her head to the side. "Michael… really?" Her tone was plain.

He laughed, nervous. "The point is… whenever Cassandra and I saw each other, it was normally one on one."

Garlic's face flashed with interest. *Oh.* "Go on," he urged.

"And, well…."

"Michael, you never got it, did you? I never went out of my way to sneak away from a father who is rash with conservative views and a mother who wants only the best for me just to play a game of hide-and-seek. I lied through my teeth whenever I could and planned my secret outings carefully just so that I could see you."

"W-what?" he stuttered.

She groaned, frustrated. "I'm saying that I've been specifically going out of my way to see you."

Oh? Garlic thought again, a small smile brewing on his fascinated face. *This is entertaining.*

"We just lacked the communication…. Did you not ever wonder why I would just turn up of my own accord?"

Michael's face paled. "That makes a disturbing amount of sense." The two stood close but with an awkward tension. Garlic grinned at them. "No one else has ever really questioned you, if I am to be fair. Brandon's the only one who lives closest and has brought it up before, but not anything like we imagined. I know I made quite the handful's worth of 'posh girl' jokes, but… well… you are from a filthy-rich family. And, not even rich, I mean—"

"Michael," she butted in, and cut him off before he could finish, "I'm sorry," she said quickly.

"No, it's okay… I have asked you about it in the past myself."

Cassandra shied away and began to tug Garlic down the stairs. Garlic took slow steps down with them and stayed close enough to hear every last word.

"Whenever you asked too many personal questions, I got weird about it for a reason, Michael."

"I just thought you had privacy issues."

"Well, yes, I suppose."

The two shared the sweet sound of laughter together, then rushed down into the cramped space together with Garlic, who stayed a pace or two ahead.

"We need to be quiet," she muttered.

"We?" he questioned, brash as he kept her close as a patrol wandered by. Two guards bickered loudly among themselves and suspected nothing as they passed by them and marched deeper into the darkness. "Anyway, you were always... what is the word for it?"

"Vague?" Cassandra prompted.

"Lying?"

She weakened. "Michael," she gasped, her tone pained. Garlic grew tense at the change in atmosphere.

"I understand. Don't worry... and I'm sorry for giving you such a troublesome time about it."

"I just... I had to be cautious. I couldn't let you get to know me too well."

"Well, you succeeded," he grumbled and tried to keep them moving for Garlic's sake, only for her to grab him back.

"We're not done."

Garlic's eyebrow rose. *Oh...?* He looked behind him. *Should I go...?*

"No, it's okay. We're done. I understand—"

"No, just... listen." She kept him close, and shouted in a delicate whisper, "I made you purposely know me based on your assumptions about me."

Michael looked at her as if she had gone mad. Garlic watched on, curious.

"Sorry, say that again?"

"I said what I said," Cassandra asserted, flustered. "If you didn't understand, then...."

Should I cut in and say it made very little sense at all? Garlic wondered.

"You've got to try and talk simply. You know?" Michael chuckled and glanced behind them to make sure no one was around. "Yeah," he mumbled, then looked back at her. "We better get moving along. I'm just going to forget whatever you tried to say."

Cassandra, not only flustered but discomposed, stood her ground. "And all I am saying is... I'm sorry. But... I'll work on it."

"Your assumptions, or mine?" Michael questioned.

This is getting boring... Garlic turned to, at last, move on down the staircase of stone into the passage.

"Mine?" she answered as if it were such an obvious answer.

"More so your father," he said, which was well-received as she grabbed him by his tattered clothing and then smirked.

"Indeed," she agreed, and then let out the slightest of surprised squeaks at his touch. Careful and calm, he gently placed his palm and fingers around her red, swollen cheek.

"I'm so sorry you've had to endure this...."

Garlic began to turn away. *I don't need to be here for the sappy part.* He waited not another moment longer to make his way with a carefree attitude down the rest of the steps and under the northern city walls. He listened to them behind him as they shared words that were important to them both.

He smiled. *They're making progress....*

Bit by bit, with every step he took, as a gentle fog from the north began to settle in over the town, Garlic unwrapped his head. One cloth after another, he peeled away what fabrics coated and protected him. It took time, and all the while the group watched on in awe as he undressed from his mummified appearance, until the rags, now worthless to him, were put to one side.

19

Cassandra and Michael caught up. In the width of the tunnels, the air somewhat thin, the group looked on with reverence at the once-bloated, homeless person. Underneath the discarded layers was a vampire with a body honed like that of a warrior, scarred and wounded from an eternity of conflict and survival.

The group's awe was silent as he passed them and then spun around to reveal his truth, which snapped their perception of him in half.

He bared his fangs as he smiled. "Thank you, all of you, for reminding me of the good in people."

"You're bald?" Andrew was the first to speak and of all things, he was almost deeply upset that it had to be his scalp.

Garlic froze.

"He's bald?" Brandon seconded, his tone a mix of emotions.

"Oh, my... I didn't expect this." Cassandra's comment was loud and clear.

"What, a twist?" Sophia asked.

"Huh," Luke muttered, confused.

"Oh," Chris added, shocked.

"Garlic's bald!" Scarlett's scream of approval and shock was enough for him.

He raised his hand to the bickering group. "Night has set, which gives me only a certain amount of time to travel the distance that I need. I am sorry if I may have to rush our goodbye."

"Why are you bald?" Andrew asked. His reality seemed shattered.

"I… choose to shave it," he said, his voice a low seethe. "You see, as you look at me now," he said and showed his body, his upper torso exposed while his lower half remained encased in tightly knit undergarments for both flexibility and speed. "I hold no tools, nor anything else. I am immortal. All I need is what I am." He presented himself and saw their eyes shimmer with curiosity. "I am not pale in the slightest. All the times I accidentally went in view of the sun, silver, or the holy cross, and simply my scars and time alive, have left me tanned."

Andrew raised his hand, and Garlic began to admire the teen's insatiable thirst for truth. "But… why bald?"

"Because a tanned, marred man who looks burned often appears strange with a head of hair that would look more appropriate on a teenager; such an appearance makes him seem a ruffled and homeless fool." He cocked his head to the side in thought. "Besides," he said, voice monotonous and fair, "I tend to grow a curly afro, and I hate how much it can get in the way. Washing it isn't any easier. In my time of being alive, being bald is just far less maintenance."

"Okay, everyone," Michael interjected before the clock chimed the fact that it was too late. "Every second he spends here answering questions is going to hurt him later on. I don't want to be rude, everyone, but this is goodbye."

Garlic, despite what sadness he felt for the group as they heard that bitter truth, was glad Michael was the one to step forward. As the oldest, even after a bumpy day, they still listened to him.

Cassandra backed his point, which led to the formation of a grand ceremony of quick and heartfelt goodbyes. This was the end for them, and he wondered as he moved around them all if he would remember their names. He knew he would in his heart, and that was why he shared unique goodbyes with them all: Luke, Christopher, Andrew, Sophia, Emma, Brenna, Abbey, Brandon, Cari, and then, finally, Scarlett.

He knelt and offered the sweet little girl with the bubbly smile and wide eyes a goodbye. She didn't shed a tear; for the most part, she was simply tired. It had been a long day for her filled with worry and stress, and now, like Cassandra's mother from so, so long ago, he hoped Scarlett would grow up with a warmer view of life.

"Goodbye, little one," he whispered and sat her down on the damp stone slabs.

"Bye, Garlic Senior!"

He grinned. *Ah, so she does remember.*

He looked to the group once more and turned to see where the tunnel led. He didn't see its end and knew Cassandra would lead him.

"We should go," Garlic said to her, and she followed. Now was the time for action. Much of the group stayed in the wide, open tunnel, feeling sad to say goodbye but happy to have experienced this, nevertheless.

Cassandra led him through the dark of the tunnel that dripped water and was coated with fog from the outside world. The pair weaved through the tunnel's intricate system until a breeze blasted inward, finding the travelers. She followed it, as did he until they reached the end. They were met by a muddied marsh, the moat of the town bringing with it a thick smell. The water was calm. The night watch on the walls called out warnings of the thick fog and how they saw nothing through it.

"This opportunity is perfect...," he turned to face Cassandra once more. "This little dock... what purpose does it serve?" he asked and looked at the shambles of what appeared to be a miniature dock with a single rowboat big enough for two people tied to the wooden poles that extended from the base of the moat's floor.

"I don't know," she answered.

He hummed and walked toward it, careful with his steps against the creaking wood whilst she stayed within the tunnel's mouth.

"Garlic," she said, and he stopped. "I have one more question."

"You are welcome to ask," he said and stood beside the rowboat.

"Your immortality... does it include eternal youth?"

He smiled at her question. "You ask well... I'll grant you this last answer. It's not eternal youth. I age, yes, but once I've reached my prime, I stay there. However, a heavy amount of activity, bad blood, exercise, perhaps drug use and wounds and injuries and.... Well, my eternal youth would be gone. When I was first cursed, I was warned to keep my health so that I would not fall into the trap of being disfigured from poor life choices forever. I am more of a scarred, tired vampire now. I look older than my prime since life has done that to me. Otherwise, I am still young, truly, and shouldn't be taken lightly."

Cassandra nodded and fiddled at her dress. "Thank you.... It's just, everyone likes the idea of being immortal. All of my friends... but I don't think they understand."

Garlic released an utterance of frustration. "I wished they wouldn't find so much 'good' in immortality. I disagree. I've watched kingdoms rise and fall, empires collapse from within—I've seen the kindest of hearts and the coldest of souls. I've seen beauty and destruction. I'm not even sure how old I am. All I know is that I've surely seen it all, and quite frankly,

I wouldn't wish this on anyone else. Yet I am terrified of death, truly. I've been alive for so long that to think if I should die, and God rejects me… then, what is next? I may as well have lived. It's not a risk I want to take, and if I should die, I want to die fighting— whoever can kill me one day will have prestige and a title unlike any other, and I like to believe I'll make their life good. I do not know. Frankly, it's a tough question, and if I could have just been a vampire without the immortality, I would have accepted the opportunity in seconds."

Cassandra, mouth agape, found nothing but a disarray of words leaving her lips. Nothing made sense. She had nothing left to offer but her comfort in the form of a blundered attempt at words. He laughed at her reaction and turned away.

"I do quite enjoy philosophy too…. I've met many who try to argue life. I feel I have some saddening answers for them."

"You must be terrified at heart… to never be able to get close with someone. Is that why you wish to leave us so soon?"

"Of course," he said, calm and stoic. "You think you're the first group who've welcomed me warmly? I've had entire communities adapt for me and make me 'domestic,' and then one day, time came for all of them too."

Cassandra nearly recoiled, unable to think of a way to provide him a good life.

"I'm sorry if I come across as cruel now in my words. I've learned after a long life that honesty is easier, always. There's no point of mystery or intrigue when I may end up ruining the other person's life, friend, or lover as they grow old and lose themselves while I remain young, unable to stop the passage of time. It has always been easier, as with the group, to acknowledge the kindness and understanding of the few who are willing to be open-minded, thank them, tell them to never change, and then move on with life."

"I understand," she said, quickly. "Please, it's okay."

His shoulders dropped, and he loosened up his tense posture. He took a stance and bowed partly. "Sandra, you and your friends have asked me many, many questions. I am sorry I cannot truly answer them all, but speak to your mother. She'll explain everything."

"What?"

"And I was curious myself. You've used the lie often enough of some form of a festival? Or was it a performance?"

Cassandra blinked. "May we reverse back to what you said before?"

"No," he answered with a grin, "but about my question…?"

Cassandra twiddled with her fingers. "There was some kind of show…. That's not a lie exactly, but…

most of it was made up. We have performing groups who sometimes during heavy trade months like to put on a sudden show for visitors. It is common for them to secretly recruit outsiders to their show. It's been quite beautiful before, really. The clash of cultures, as they say…."

Garlic nodded. "And how much of it was true?"

"I don't know, to be honest. I've used the theatre organization as a way to lie to my parents before, and they never pry for details to avoid spoiling things. They do, however, donate money. It's… a win for everyone in the end. If my parents ask again, I'll mention that there was a cancellation."

Garlic looked away from her. "Ah, well… that's the last of any questions I might've had."

"Then, wait. What did you mean by ask my mother before?"

"Garlic!" a shrill cry echoed down the tunnel.

20

"Scarlett, be quiet!" Michael could be heard from not far behind.

Garlic, who had barely moved to put his foot down in the boat, bounced back against the creaking wooden dock. He spun and saw the little girl hobble out into the fog of the dock.

"Please don't mind her. She just had one more question," Michael mentioned, nearly knocking into Cassandra as he rushed, followed by a swarm of shouting behind him. The group charged through the narrow quarters to find some kind of wiggle room for whatever it was Scarlett wanted.

Garlic watched the group in envy and appreciated Brandon's hardly subtle attempt to push Michael and Cassandra together. The eager group watched on.

"I am sorry for rambling on...." He turned away. "Thank you, everyone." He stepped into the rowboat and plopped down as it rocked and rattled against the water. "You have all proved to be heroes, and Sandra," he said, his final words meant for the person who least expected it. "Please," he begged softly, "tell your mother that I am thankful and will one day visit again."

Finally, he looked up at Scarlett, who stood taller than him from where she stood on the dock. "Yes, Scarlett?" he asked her sweetly.

She opened her mouth, and out came proud stuttering. "Are-are-are you a villain or a hero?"

A final question.

He smiled. "In tales, you will hear the perspective of heroes and villains, and a true hero is someone who is not only true to themselves but will act without thought when saving another's life. This is a natural thing, most likely, as those who try to act like a hero even if it is not who they are at heart will usually fail. A hero is more often born, in my eyes, and sometimes made…." He saw Scarlett's bewilderment. He knew all she wanted was a straight answer. After this moment, he knew he would likely never see them again. Only time would tell for sure. "Alas, for me? Well, I am whatever you believe me to be."

New Book Releases

Thank you for reading *Saving Garlic*! Be sure to check out our other books at:

twistedkeypublishing.com

Follow F. Lockhaven on Amazon and Goodreads to learn about new releases and giveaways.

Other books by F. Lockhaven

Short Stories

The Magical Amulet

Savior of Dragons

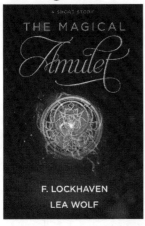

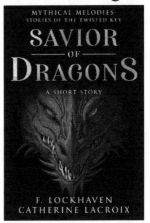

YA Fantasy Adventure

The Living Lore: The
Shades of the Abyss

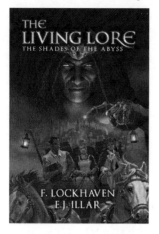

YA Dystopian

PanTech Chronicles:
Shadowfalcon

F. Lockhaven is one of Grace Lockhaven's author pen names, primarily focused on Teen and Young Adult Science Fiction and Fantasy. If you love reading Premature Teen Fantasy stories, you may enjoy reading her other stories:

The Secret Fountain

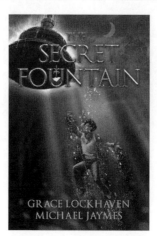

Quest Chasers

The Deadly Cavern
Book 1

The Screaming Mummy
Book 2

The Ghosts of Ian Stanley

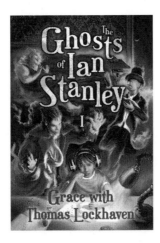

Manufactured by Amazon.ca
Bolton, ON

20046258R00120